Penguin Science Fiction
The Productions of Tim

John Brunner was born in Oxfordshire in 1934. His acquaintance with science fiction began at the age of six, when 'someone misguidedly left a copy of *The War of the Worlds* in the nursery'. While still at school in 1951 he sold his first paperback novel ('mercifully it appeared under a pseudonym and sank without trace'), and during the following year made his first sales to American S F magazines.

After his R.A.F. service he worked for a while as a technical abstractor on a magazine edited by the S F writer John Christopher, and then as a publisher's editor in the same office as S F writer Jonathan Burke. Since the end of 1958 he has been a freelance.

He has sold well over fifty books – novels, short novels and story collections – the majority of them being science fiction. Three of his novels, including *The Squares of the City* and *Telepathist* (also available in Penguins), have been shortlisted for the annual best S F novel award, the 'Hugo', which he received in 1949 for *Stand on Zanzibar*. A play adapted from his story *Some Lapse of Time* topped the viewers' panel ratings for the first of B.B.C. TV's 'Out of the Unknown' series. In 1966 he was made the first recipient of the British Fantasy Award; in 1967 he was Guest of Honour at the annual British S F Convention; and in 1970 he won the British Science Fiction Association Award.

He and his wife Marjorie live in Hampstead, London. His interests include folksong, writing topical and satirical verse, and touring Britain and Europe in his sports convertible. A good deal of his time is devoted to administering the Martin Luther King Memorial Prize, which he founded within a few days of Dr King's assassination.

John Brunner

The Productions of Time

Penguin Books

Penguin Books Ltd, Harmondsworth,
Middlesex, England
Penguin Books Australia Ltd, Ringwood,
Victoria, Australia

First published in the U.S.A. by New American Library 1967
Published in Penguin Books 1970

Made and printed in Great Britain
by C. Nicholls & Company Ltd
Set in Linotype Times

Eternity is in love with the productions of time.
WILLIAM BLAKE: *The Marriage of Heaven and Hell*

1

Precisely because the idea made him nervous, Murray Douglas rang the Proscenium Restaurant and booked a table for lunch before going to bail out his car. The man who took his reservation was a stranger, by his voice, and there was no hint of recognition when he repeated the instructions he had been given.

'Mr Murray Douglas – table for one – one o'clock. Very good, sir.'

It had been a long time. It had been an eternity.

His hand was shaking as he cradled the phone. To bring himself back under control, he drew a deep breath and let it out slowly, steadily, as though trying to sustain a level note on a musical instrument. For the twentieth time, he pressed the inside of his wrist against the front of his jacket, to verify the thick solidity of the hundred pounds in his wallet. Then he shrugged on his overcoat, picked up his travelling bag, gave a last look around the apartment, and went down to the street to find a taxi.

The garage, at least, hadn't changed. Tom Hickie was still in his little glass-sided office surrounded by stacks of grease-marked service sheets and continually ringing phones. The air was still full of crackling radio music and the bang of hammers. He picked his way between the ranks of cars, stepping over air-lines and wheeled heavy-duty jacks.

Phone in one hand, papers in the other, Hickie glanced around as the door slid back. For a moment he was puzzled. Then he caught himself.

'Oh, it's Mr Douglas! It's been such a long time, sir, I almost didn't recognize you.'

'You got my letter?' Murray said roughly. He didn't like to think about the long time or about people not recognizing him. The mirror had told him too much already. Last time he called here, he had already begun to lose the youthful handsomeness on which he had built so much of his reputation and following; his cheeks were fuller then, his eyes were growing watery and there were always pouches under them.

But now he had really changed. There was slack skin along the line of his jaw. There were old-man's furrows in his forehead. And he had a hat crammed low on his head because his scalp was showing at the crown and there was grey everywhere. Murray Douglas at thirty-two looked fifty and felt a hundred.

'Yes, sir – we got your letter, and the boys are bringing the car out now. We've looked after her for you, you may be sure of that.' Hickie put down the phone he was holding and a glint of curiosity showed in his eyes. 'I gather you've been ill, sir. I was very sorry to hear about it. I hope you've made a good recovery.'

Abruptly Murray was sick of the polite fiction his agent had circulated. He said, 'The hell! I haven't been ill – I've been in a sanatorium to stop me from drinking myself to death.'

Hickie's mouth, opening to say something further, stayed open for a long moment. Then he looked uncomfortably down at his table of service sheets.

'I'm sorry, Mr Douglas. I didn't mean to be nosy.'

'That's all right.' Murray felt in his pocket for his cigarette case; there were big NO SMOKING signs up, but no one took much notice of them. 'Cigarette?'

'No thank you, sir. I'm trying to give it up.' Hickie essayed a casual laugh which turned into a croak. 'Ah! Here comes Bill now to say your car is ready.' He moved past Murray in the doorway.

Bill, a tall West Indian in brown overalls, called out as he approached. 'The Daimler's ready, Mr Hickie. I just took the job sheet in to be costed.'

'Good!' Hickie said. 'So we won't keep you long, Mr Douglas.'

'How is the car?' Murray demanded.

'Your Daimler, boss?' Bill turned to him. 'Well, we had a fair amount of work to do on it. Excuse my saying so, but you drive your cars damned hard.'

'I used to,' Murray muttered. 'I used to drive myself too.'

'Sorry, boss?' Bill widened his eyes anxiously. 'Didn't hear that?'

'Never mind.' Murray felt for his wallet. 'How much do I owe you for storage, Tom?'

At first, being back in the driving seat and hearing the beautiful even purr of the V-8 under the downswept bonnet helped to mask even the painful knowledge that Hickie had literally not known who he was when he first appeared. He drove cautiously through the West End towards St Martin's Lane and the Proscenium.

But things had changed here, too. There were new one-way signs, and the pavements had sprouted parking meters. By the time he had wasted a quantity of petrol and a good half hour of time creeping around traffic-throttled side streets in search of a vacant space to leave the car, he was back in the mood of depression in which he had spent most of the past few months. What the hell was the point of going to the Proscenium, anyway? A silly theatrical gesture. A shout: 'Murray Douglas is back!' To get what response? A few raised eyebrows, maybe, and a snide, 'So what?'

Blazes, but I'm going through with it. I've backed down and backed out too often. I've spent too long on the easy road.

He finally found a place for the car and made his way, sullen-faced, to the restaurant.

Emile, the head waiter, recognized him, but even his professional smile could not wholly hide his shock at the change which a year had wrought. And he had another reason for distress.

'I'm very sorry, Mr Douglas,' he was saying. 'But your reservation was for one o'clock, I believe. When at half-past one you had not arrived, I am afraid . . .' And he made a gesture to complete the sentence.

Now if you'd done that in the old days, I'd have created a scene. But you wouldn't have dared to do it then. Now you think I'm washed up . . .

Murray forced himself to swallow his resentment. He said, 'I've wasted about half an hour looking for a parking place. I'm sorry if I inconvenienced you, Emile. Never mind – you can fit me in somewhere, I suppose.'

'Ah – There is only one empty table, Mr Douglas.' Emile pointed somewhere towards the back of the crowded restaurant. 'François will attend to you. François, show Mr Douglas to his table, please. Yes, Mr Crombie, I'll be with you in a moment!'

Puzzled glances ('I'm sure I know who that is, but –!') followed him through the restaurant. None of the people who looked up was known to him; there were several people here whom he did know, of course, but he was glad that every single one of his former friends was too busy eating or talking to notice his passage. The table he was given was blessedly inconspicuous, half screened by a bank of the luscious indoor creepers the designer of the place had been so fond of. At the next table, around a corner and in an alcove, were two men whose voices he immediately recognized – Pat Burnett, the drama critic of the *Gazette*, and Ralph Heston-Wood of *Acting*.

They hadn't noticed his arrival. They were deep in discussion of a rehearsal they had just seen. Murray sat listening with intense concentration, thinking himself back into the past.

God, but he missed it all! Why had he been such a fool as to come here alone instead of calling his agent? Roger would have been glad to –

No, probably he wouldn't, and no use kidding myself. Not after the months of hanging around; not after the endless loans, the savage complaints, the moans of despair.

Since coming out of the sanatorium, since hanging around and hoping when there was no hope, Murray Douglas had become far better acquainted with Murray Douglas.

And I don't like Murray Douglas very much.

With as much delight as a man fresh from jail (and those abominable snack bars had been a kind of jail), he studied the menu and picked some favourites: avocado pear, *truite au bleu*.

'And for wine?' the wine steward asked.

'Apple juice,' Murray said curtly. 'Chilled.'

He lit a cigarette and leaned back, waiting for the food to arrive.

Now the two critics at the next table had switched to a different subject. At first he only let his attention drift idly back to them. Suddenly, as Murray heard what they were saying, he was all ears.

'What do you make of this man Delgado, Ralph – this Argentinian that Blizzard's got hold of?'

'Oh, he has something, there's no doubt of it,' Heston-Wood answered. 'Didn't you see the thing he did in Paris with Jean-Paul Garrigue? *Trois Fois à la Fois,* I think he called it.'

'No, I didn't see it, and from all accounts it wasn't my cup of tea anyway,' Burnett grunted.

Heston-Wood gave a chuckle. 'Yes, I remember what you had to say about *The Connection,* Pat! What was the rhyme they were passing around – "Hail, stale disciple of the tried and true" – something like that?'

'That was one of Maxie's. Nobody minds Maxie. Seriously, Ralph, what the blazes is the point of all this nonsense? If you have a play you have a play and there's an author who put it together. But from what I can gather, this *isn't* a play. There's a fast-talking dago with an avant-garde label on him who's conned Blizzard into vouching for him and someone else into putting up one hell of a lot of money, and a gang of no-goods, has-beens, and deadbeats scraped off the bottom of the barrel because no one in his right mind will touch the job.'

Murray felt a thick constricting band of anger close around his heart.

'Pat, you carry this theatre-for-the-masses pose a bit too far sometimes. You haven't even seen Delgado's work, and you're condemning it out of hand.' Heston-Wood drank noisily. 'The one he did with Garrigue gave me the most stimulating evening I've had in a theatre since *Godot*.'

'It didn't run,' Burnett said.

'No. Well, there was Garrigue's suicide, you know.'

'Yes, but for heaven's sake! Rest in peace and all that – that's a publicity gimmick to end all gimmicks. Why didn't it go on with a replacement?'

'Because the piece was created around a specific cast, and a replacement would have destroyed it. There *is* a point to the idea, Pat. You just won't see it.'

'I know all about that. Saroyan was over here a few years back, remember? He tried the same thing at Theatre Workshop. I thought it was abysmal nonsense, and I said so.' There was a sound of clinking glass as Burnett poured more wine. 'You get your cast together and get a few basic suggestions, and you work up your dialogue co-operatively, and you call the result a play. But get a masterpiece out of this bunch of second-rate hams? You'll never make me swallow that, Ralph. Why, there's nobody better in the whole gang of them than Murray Douglas, and you know as well as I do he's turned into such a gin-swilling sot there isn't a producer in London who'd look at him. And he never had real talent anyway – just a pretty face.'

Murray stood up. He didn't bother to push the table away; its legs scraped, it half tilted and spilled a couple of knives off its edge before settling back on an even keel. With his face absolutely white, he went around the concealing screen of greenery.

There was a clang as Heston-Wood dropped his fork on his plate. It was the last noise. A total silence seemed to have invaded the restaurant, lasting only heartbeats – but that was enough.

Burnett, his lower lip visibly shaking, stared up at Murray as though at a ghost. He was a big, burly man with a ruddy face. His gimmick, carefully husbanded by his editor, was what Heston-Wood had called 'theatre for the masses', and the picture that ran at the head of his column showed him grinning around a Priestley-type meerschaum pipe.

'Get up,' Murray said.

'Now – now look here, Murray!'

Murray reached out and took him by the knot of his tie. His

rage lent him strength he had never had and after the wreck he had made of his body was not entitled to. He dragged Burnett to his feet and sent his chair over with a crash. Then he hit him as hard as he could under the jaw.

The burly man staggered backwards and collapsed on the table of another party, planting one hand in a plate of crème caramel. Ignoring the cries of alarm and shouts from waiters which now went up, Murray drew a deep breath.

'Somebody ought to have done that to you years ago, Burnett. Hear me, you ignorant slob? You're not a critic and you never will be. You're a foul-minded gossip columnist with the morals of a baboon and the bad taste of a whole hen party of Aunt Ednas. I wanted to kick your teeth in a hundred times when I was on top of the tree, and I didn't dare because of the power your dirty little column gives you. Now I'm back at the bottom, and you can't hurt me. But you go on trying, don't you? You called me a gin-swilling sot, isn't that right? All right, now's your chance to say it again *knowing* I can hear you!'

Panting heavily, Burnett straightened up. He mouthed some sort of apology to the owner of the sticky sweet in which he had planted his hand.

'Mr Douglas! *Bon Dieu*, what have you done?' From the front of the restaurant came Emile, as agitated as only an interruption of his smooth routine could make him.

'It's all right, Emile. I'm leaving. If I'd known I was going to be under the same roof as Burnett I wouldn't have come in. The sight of him spoils my appetite.' Murray spoke with the full resonance of his trained voice, the voice which had once been able to fill the monstrous volume of the Albert Hall without a microphone, and knew that everyone could hear every word. 'Take that for any damage I've done to your property!' He peeled a five-pound note off the wad remaining in his wallet, and dug in his pocket as he continued. 'And you can take this for your damage, Burnett.'

He flipped a single penny contemptuously through the air towards the burly man. It landed on the carpet between his feet. He turned his back and walked slowly towards the door, aware that this time every customer in the place was watching him and nobody was any longer asking who *that* might be.

The best exit I've made for a long while, he thought bitterly.

'Murray!'

He paused and glanced around. At a table near the door he saw Fleet Dickinson, who was more on top than anybody and never likely to be anywhere else. The full charm turned on high.

'Murray, I'm damned glad to see you back in the land of the living, and congratulations on what you just did to Patsy-boy. What are you doing at the moment? Hardly heard a word of you since – well, you know.' A twist of a graceful hand in the air.

'Since they wrung the gin out,' Murray said flatly. 'Why, I've been resting. On doorsteps, mainly. I tried to get in to see you, too, and one of the doorsteps I rested on was yours.'

A flicker of well-controlled embarrassment. 'Well, Murray, you know how it is when something like this happens.'

'I know only too intimately how it is. Don't let me spoil your lunch, will you? So long.'

'Just a moment – uh – Murray!'

He paused and looked back.

'Look, if you're really in difficulties –'

'Not any more, thanks. Blizzard picked me for this gang of no-goods, deadbeats, and has-beens he's collecting for the new Delgado play, so I'm provided for. See you in the stalls when we open.'

That was a childish sort of jab to end with, Murray told himself as he went back on the street. The damnable thing was, of course, that he was just as suspicious as Burnett of the whole Delgado project, and if his agent had been able to find him anything else – anything at all – he wouldn't have considered it even for the fantastic rates of pay.

2

His mind clouded by what had happened, he picked his way north through London towards the southern end of the M1 motorway. He pulled up once in order to take the top of the

car down – he felt that he needed some fresh air to blow Burnett out of his memory – and to buy a sandwich instead of the good lunch he'd left behind at the Proscenium.

So far, he'd been driving cautiously; he hadn't touched the wheel of anything but a slowpoke family saloon since the onset of his breakdown. Once he hit the motorway however, he deliberately took the car up to the maximum of its performance, holding third gear until the hundred and ten showed, then shifting to top and letting her roll.

Even if it was only for advancing him the cash to ransom the car from storage, Murray was grateful to Manuel Delgado.

He hadn't disposed of the Daimler because in the end it had come to be a potent symbol to him. The registration plates said 1 MQD for Murray Quest Douglas; people recognized it on the street, the white SP 250 with the black flashes down the sides – 'There's Murray Douglas in that car! I saw a shot of it on TV last week!'

Once, held up beside him in a traffic jam, a taxi driver had passed a sheet of paper over from his cab asking for an autograph.

Maybe he'd been bloody-minded about it. He could have raised seven or eight hundred on it, even though, as Bill the mechanic had said, it had been driven hard, and he wouldn't have had to eat so many meals out of cans or switch to a brand of cigarettes that tasted of horsedung or wear an unpressed suit to useless interviews. Roger Grady had told him often enough he was a fool to let the car sit in store with the charges mounting week by week; he'd still been going on about it even when he broke the incredible news – that Sam Blizzard was putting together a cast for Delgado and wanted Murray Douglas if he'd accept.

His mind roamed back over that curious talk with Roger.

He'd heard of Delgado, naturally. The playwright was of Argentine origin. There had been a film, at a time when the only South American name to ring bells with the cognoscenti had been Leopoldo Torre-Nilsson. Murray hadn't seen it – it had only been screened at a film festival, and no circuit would book it for general showing – but he knew people who had, and those people said it was phenomenal. A *comédie noire* to end *comédies noires*.

He'd come to Europe on the strength of his reputation from that film, and last year Jean-Paul Garrigue, one of the finest young actors in Paris, had taken the leading role in the experimental production which Burnett and Heston-Wood had been talking about. Again, Murray hadn't seen it; he'd already been in the sanatorium by then. But he'd read the notices, and some of them had been raves.

Then there was Garrigue's suicide, and a sensation, and for months on end, silence. As though Garrigue's depression had been contagious, Delgado no longer seemed to enthuse anyone.

And then Roger's news.

'Will I accept?' Murray echoed, looking around at the sleek furniture of the agent's office as though thinking on his awakening it might disappear. 'Blizzard asks for me personally and I'm going to hesitate? Are you crazy, Roger?'

'Well, I know some people who would,' Roger said after a pause.

'Why? For heaven's sake, they were raving about Delgado in Paris last year!'

'Yes, they were.' Roger looked down at the end of his cigar with intent concentration. 'You've been pretty well out of the swim since then, of course. Sort of not plugged into the grapevine, what I mean. I'm not saying I'm not delighted, mark you, and if the project's a success no one could possibly deserve it more than you after the way you've pulled yourself together. But I wouldn't be honest if I didn't warn you that there *are* people around – I could name them – who wouldn't take a part in a Delgado play if you paid them a thousand pounds a day.'

'Why on earth not?'

'Because Garrigue killed himself. Because Léa Martinez went into an asylum. Because Claudette Myrin tried to murder her baby daughter.' Roger wasn't kidding. His voice was level and his face was straight.

'I didn't know about the girls,' Murray said. 'They were in the Paris production, weren't they? But look, if I get you right, you're saying that there are some superstitious folk in the business who think there's a jinx on Delgado.'

'More or less.'

'Did you ever know me to be superstitious, Roger?'

'No.' Roger sighed. 'Still, I had to warn you. Matter of fact, I was talking about this project with someone only yesterday and got a flat no before I made any offer at all. I wasn't going to make an offer – Blizzard has some screwball idea of who he does and doesn't want –'

'Meaning me, Roger?' Murray cut in.

'No. To be honest, no. Did you ever know me to loan four hundred quid to someone I thought was really washed up? My business instinct wouldn't permit it. No, I'm sure you have it in you to get back in the game – and maybe do even better because you won't have your handsome juvenile face to cover your failings.' Roger could speak more frankly to Murray than anyone else in the world. 'But you're the only one of the bunch so far who strikes me as being on the credit side. However, I'm not in charge, and Blizzard has a head as hard as anyone I know. Besides, even if the damn thing comes to town and folds after four nights, it's giving you a chance to turn in something the critics will notice.'

'What you really mean is it'll stop me pestering you for a few weeks,' Murray said sourly.

'You've been a bloody nuisance, Murray, and you've run up a bloody sizeable debt with me. More than once, you've accused me of not doing my best for you, and I'd have kicked you down the stairs if I hadn't known – well, what I do know. You don't enjoy struggling, boy, and don't you let other people see it!'

'All right, can it,' Murray said. It was true, what Roger was saying, and despite the agent's light tone it hurt. 'Give me the details. And the pay doesn't matter. Right now, I'll take a second standard-bearer at minimum rate.'

'You'll get a bit more than that. There's money in this, boy, Blizzard's taken over a bankrupt country club called Fieldfare House, up Bedford way, and he's planning to have the cast there – all expenses paid – until he brings the show into London. The idea is for it to follow *Amaranth* into the Margrave; you know *Amaranth* is getting pretty rocky. If there's time, there'll be a week's pre-London try-out, probably at the New Brecht, but more than likely you'll be at the Margrave four weeks from now.'

'Did you say *four* weeks?'

'No, Blizzard said it. You take it up with him, boy. You'll have plenty of opportunity – you're going to this club of his on Friday.'

Friday, an hour earlier than expected because he had gone without his lunch, Murray swung the nose of the car past the faded sign indicating Fieldfare House.

3

A winding gravelled drive led from the narrow hedge-lined road up to the house. The grounds must have played a part in reducing the club to bankruptcy, Murray guessed. They were extremely elaborate, and even before he stopped at the front entrance he had seen a maze of carefully tended box, magnificent ranks of rhododendrons, beds of what looked like peonies set among neglected lawns. Around the corner of the house he glimpsed the high board of a swimming pool.

The house was a rambling structure of grey stone and old brick, with dark red creepers reaching to the roof. It had an empty look; the windows were dirty, and one of the ground-floor rooms was shuttered. There was a gravelled stand for cars at the left of the front door, which boasted a pillared porch no less than seven stone steps of decreasing width.

He pulled up, switched off the engine, and in the sudden silence had to repress a wild thought – that this was an alcoholic delusion, and Blizzard had never asked for him at all, and he had come to a deserted house to find nobody waiting and no hope for the future.

He snatched the key from the ignition and jumped out. With as much noise as possible he slammed the car's door and opened the boot. He reached inside for his travelling bag.

'You will be Mr Murray Douglas.'

The voice was as soft and unexpected as if the trees had spoken to him. He started violently and let the lid of the boot fall with a crash. At his elbow a man of indeterminate age and nationality, wearing a black suit and a black tie, had appeared like a conjuring trick. He hadn't even made a crunching sound in the gravel as he approached.

Conscious of prickly sweat on his spine, Murray said, 'Yes, I am. You seem to be – uh – expecting me.'

'Yes, sir. My name is Valentine, and I am the head steward here. May I take your bag and show you to your accommodations?'

The extraordinary Victorian phrase heightened instead of dispelling Murray's sense of unreality. He stared at Valentine, taking in the pale, unlined, ageless face, with its dark eyes, the immaculate suit like a funeral mute's, the high-sided black leather boots in which the legs terminated.

'Your bag, sir?'

'Oh – here you are. Is Mr Blizzard here yet?'

'No, sir. You are the first to arrive. I expect Mr Blizzard at six o'clock and Mr Delgado with him. The rest of the company will be arriving at various times this afternoon or this evening. Please come this way.'

He turned. Even the weight of the bag didn't seem to make his footsteps grind the gravel. Feeling as though he was walking beside a ghost, Murray accompanied him up the steps, through a small vestibule inside the front door, and into a large – no, an enormous – hall. It reached up to an arched ceiling and a domed skylight, and a gallery serving the upper rooms ran around it from a curving staircase with a polished mahogany balustrade. There were the country club's ornaments and decorations everywhere: old sporting prints, horse brasses, foxes' masks and brushes, a pair of eighteenth-century fowling pieces with the barrels polished like silver, a tiger skin in front of the roast-an-ox fireplace.

Valentine led him upstairs, but instead of turning along the gallery, opened a green baize door at the head of the staircase and went through it. Beyond stretched a long light corridor, with panels of fluted glass let into its ceiling and numbered doors on either side. This must be a new wing jutting from the back of the house, which Murray hadn't seen as he drove up.

'Your room, sir,' Valentine said, putting a key in the furthest door. 'Number fourteen.'

There was a room thirteen adjacent, Murray noticed. He wondered idly whether it was going to be left vacant, in view of the number of theatrical people who were superstitious, or whether he was going to find himself with a doggedly sceptical neighbour for the duration of his stay. Then, as he followed the steward into his own 'accommodations', he forgot the question. He couldn't prevent himself whistling.

Many London hotels would be glad of a few rooms like this. Plain, square, low-ceilinged, it was panelled with maple and raw yellow pine. A low double divan with a smoke-grey candlewick cover on it was flanked by twin bedside tables, one of which bore a phone, the other a huge vase of flowers. A full-size Picasso reproduction was centred over the head of the bed. The windows, curtained with dark green hessian, ran the length of the outside wall and gave a view on to the lawn behind the house and dark woods beyond. The corner of the swimming pool was just visible. There was a TV set on a white iron stand, an easy chair, a shelf bearing a row of *Readers' Union* editions and a stack of back numbers of *Acting*.

Add one to the list of reasons why the club went broke. Murray gave an impressed nod and wandered to peer out of the window. At a half-seen movement behind him, he turned back; Valentine was opening his bag, which he hadn't locked, as it was riding with him in the car, and had started to lay out his belongings.

'No, leave that, Valentine,' Murray said. 'I prefer to sort out my own gear. Here.' He felt for a tip, but Valentine raised a pale hand to prevent him.

'That's not necessary, sir. Mr Blizzard is giving me a very generous retainer.'

'Oh. I see.' Murray shrugged and dropped the coins back in his pocket. 'Say, what's the routine going to be – have you a timetable of some sort?' He took the first few items from his bag and began to sort them into groups on the bed.

'I understand that it will be up to Mr Delgado and the progress which is made with the play, sir. Tonight there is to be dinner at seven-thirty, after which Mr Delgado wishes to make the acquaintance of everyone present, and there will be some kind of an introductory discussion.'

'I see. Are you left over from the country club they used to have here, by the way?' Murray put socks and shirts into a handy drawer, picked up a spare suit on its hanger and went to the tall built-in wardrobe beyond the bed.

'No, sir. I am specially retained by Mr Blizzard. I'm as much a stranger as yourself.'

'Doing things in style, isn't he – old Blizzard?' Murray made to close the wardrobe door; in the act, he froze, staring down at something half seen on the lowermost shelf at the side of the cupboard. He barely caught Valentine's reply.

'I wouldn't know, sir. I'm not acquainted with the world of the theatre. Is something wrong, sir?'

Murray forced himself out of his trance. 'Yes,' he confirmed grimly. 'This is wrong.' He tugged open the other door of the wardrobe and picked up what had caught his eye. He handed it to Valentine – a full, unopened bottle of White Horse.

'And this! And this! And this!' One after the other, he snatched up bottles – Booth's Dry London gin, Lemon Hart rum, Cognac Hennessy. There were glasses there, too, a syphon of soda and bottles of lime and orange squash – but those were safe. He was sweating as he faced Valentine again, whose arms cradled the liquor and whose features were carefully composed into an expression of polite inquiry.

'Get rid of them,' he instructed curtly. 'Is that part of Blizzard's orders – laying in that stock for me?'

'Mr Blizzard did require me to provide suitable refreshment in the visitors' rooms, yes.'

'All right, forget it. Just get rid of the stuff. Suitable refreshment for me is – oh, damnation! Get me a dozen cans of fruit juice.'

'Very good, sir.' If Valentine understood why he was being snapped at, he didn't let it show. 'Will that be all for the moment?'

'Yes. Definitely all.'

It was going to be tough. But he'd always known that. At the sanatorium they'd told him, sympathetically but without sentimental pity, that it might be years before he dared take even a glass of beer; that he'd have to achieve a plateau of emotional stability from which he couldn't slip back into his personal slough of despond. They'd said, in so many words, that if he took a drop of alcohol before he'd put five years of professional success and personal adjustment behind him, he would go to the gutter and stay there.

Murray Douglas didn't like Murray Douglas very much. But in the gutter he'd hate him.

He had a store of tranquillizers they'd given him at the sanatorium, still not quite exhausted. He dug the packet out from the bottom of his bag and looked around for water. In the corner of the room was a washbasin with a mirrored cupboard over it. He cupped his hand under the cold tap, collecting enough water to rinse down the pill, and in a few minutes felt much better.

The rest of his gear, he decided, could wait till later. For the moment, he wanted to get acquainted with the setup he'd landed in.

Valentine, he found, had left the key in the outside of his door. He locked the door and set off on his tour of inspection.

The interior of the house didn't detain him long. The big hall he had come through gave on to a dining room, a lounge with a bar in one corner, a reading room, and several other rooms whose doors were locked. He judged that one of the locked doors must give access to kitchens and storerooms. He left the door which led back into the new wing until last; it opened easily and he found beyond it not the corridor he had expected, but a complete small theatre with about sixty seats, a projection booth with a pair of sixteen-mill Bell and Howells, and a very decent-sized stage.

He whistled under his breath. So Blizzard did know what he was doing! Facilities like these weren't found under bushes. Abruptly, the idea of high-pressuring a London production from scratch in four weeks didn't seem so ridiculous after all. Author, cast, producer – and presumably lighting engineer, set designer and so on – under one roof, with their own miniature theatre for the rehearsals! That could be far, far better and more productive than meeting for rehearsal and then dispersing.

Murray cocked an eyebrow at the little theatre and went out again.

He wandered back through the big hall, catching a glimpse as he went of a man he at first thought was Valentine but who he realized after a second must be another steward, slightly taller, with the same eerie soft tread and the same mourning-black clothes. The front door was standing ajar. He paused by his car to put the top up because there was a scent of rain in the cool air, and went around the house to look at the grounds behind.

They were lavish. He crossed a long lawn, put his head into a dusty-smelling shed full of sports equipment, wandered to the edge of the swimming pool – the changing huts, too, had a dusty scent in them – and came at last to the woods beyond which he had seen from his room. They were dense and dark and very quiet. Kicking at a pebble, he followed a narrow path among the trees. He had gone barely fifty yards, and was already out of sight of the house because the path wound so, when he came to a fence.

It was eight feet tall, made of heavy-gauge linked wire on galvanized metal posts and topped with three strands of barbed wire into the bargain. There was no way of telling whether it was the club's or belonged to the owner of the adjacent property; he guessed it must be the club's, possibly installed to prevent members wandering on to other people's land.

He shrugged and turned back. There was plenty of space open to him, and he didn't care what happened beyond the fence.

At the back of his mind was the idea that it was a shame he had had to come here to work. This would have been a hell of a place to rest up after his spell in the sanatorium – if he'd had the money for it.

He was getting close to the house when he heard a car approaching up the driveway beyond. He hurried his steps; he was eager to know who else Blizzard had roped in to enjoy such unasked-for luxury.

4

It had occurred to him as he was telling Valentine to get rid of the liquor from his room that it might be difficult to withstand the offer of a drink to celebrate when everyone came together for dinner. By half past eight, when dinner was over and the dozen-odd members of the company had moved to the big lounge for what Valentine had called the introductory discussion, he was really tempted to drown his sorrows.

Somehow, he managed to distract himself as Valentine and his two aides – equally silent, identically garbed – moved in response to calls for drinks. The bar in the corner had been opened before dinner, and its stock was visibly lower now. The air was getting thick with smoke; someone had found records and put them on the player in the corner, and the chatter was loud and bright. It was more like the early stages of a party than a business meeting.

Only Murray sat sombrely by himself in a deep wing chair, his big-knuckled hands cradling a glass of limejuice and soda. His brows were ferociously drawn together as he looked and listened.

Most of the talk concerned the usual commonplaces – backbiting, sickly praise, the disgusting habits of critics. No one had said anything about Murray's own assault on Pat Burnett, and he was glad. Probably Heston-Wood had talked his colleague out of taking the matter further. It would get to people as gossip sooner or later, but at least it hadn't been in the evening papers.

Occasionally, there was a fierce burst of argument concerning a subject of real interest: the profitability of this whole idea and the value of collecting improvisation as a basis for a play. That was a point Murray had given much thought to in the past few days, and he'd expected to be discussing it seriously by now. But he didn't have the heart. He'd seen whom else Blizzard had collected, and he felt contaminated.

Blizzard himself and Delgado hadn't been at the dinner table. Valentine had conveyed, in answer to repeated questions, that they wanted to talk over some business matters and settle last-minute problems, so they were dining in another room. That rang false to Murray. It seemed more probable that Delgado was trying to build a phony aura of mystery around himself. No one here had seen him yet.

Not that anybody appeared to mind. They were quite contented with excellent food and inexhaustible liquor thrown into the deal. 'All expenses paid' was an understatement.

His eyes roamed the room. The noisier of the two small groups into which they had sorted themselves, numbered five, and included four people with whom he had previously worked. There was Ida Marr, red-haired, still slim but showing her age around her eyes and on her throat; she was posing consciously – but then, she was never really off-stage. On one side of her sat Gerry Hoading, looking incredibly boyish, younger even than his actual age of twenty-four, his fair hair untidy and his thin face propped on one upturned hand. Hoading presumably was going to be their designer; he had considerable talent, undoubtedly, but . . .

On the other side of Ida was Adrian Gardner, running a little to fat, blowing his large nose frequently into a red silk handkerchief. Murray had worked with him in *Skeleton* and knew he was a good average actor. Again – but . . .

He'd worked with Constant Baines in rep, nearly ten years ago. Constant was sitting beside Adrian, not saying much. He had stayed in rep when Murray had reached the West End; it had been something of a shock to meet him here, and their greeting had not been cordial.

And the last one of the five. Ida made a crack which Murray failed to catch, they all laughed, and the girl sitting on a cushion at Ida's feet looked up. Ida caught the movement and put her red-nailed hand on the girl's hair for a quick caress.

Her latest conquest, presumably. Shame. Murray's scowl deepened. He didn't know the girl and imagined she must be from a provincial rep somewhere; at dinner he had heard her addressed as Heather. She would be no older than twenty, he guessed. Her hair was raven black and her face was just imperfect enough to be piquant. In a plain red dress, her figure was extremely interesting.

Shame.

Murray shrugged. There was a stir and a break in the conversation, and he realized the door had opened and Blizzard had come in, followed by a sallow man who could only be the celebrated Manuel Delgado himself.

Blizzard, portly, dark-suited, waving an immense cigar, plunged forward, distributing greetings like largesse. 'Ida darling, delighted! Why, Murray! I'm so glad you could be with this venture of ours! And little Heather – how you doing so far, sweetie?'

But no one paid more than mechanical attention. They were staring at Delgado.

Makes a change, Murray thought cynically. *A cat may look ...*

There was a cold expression on the author's face. Like a snake's? Yes, Murray decided after a second's hesitation. A sort of reptilian tautness, as though his dark eyes were lidless. He was of medium height, medium build; his hair was dark, and he wore a dark blue jacket, charcoal trousers, and a grey and white tie secured by a gold bar. He held himself easily. One might have taken him more readily for an actor than – say – Constant Baines, who looked like an unsuccessful clerk.

For a long moment Murray's eyes met those peculiar snake-like dark ones. Murray felt as though he were being weighed in a balance. Then the man's stare moved on, and Murray saw he was doing the same thing to each person in turn – locking eyes with them, waiting, looking away.

Murray felt another pang of disillusionment. The word for this wasn't *phony*. It was *cheap*.

'All right, everybody!' Blizzard had moved to a table at the side of the room and parked himself on a large chair behind it, where he could face the others. 'Manuel?'

Delgado nodded and walked around the table to another chair beside Blizzard's. He went gracefully. A thought crossed Murray's mind, and he glanced sidelong at Adrian Gardner. As he'd thought, Ade's eyes were following that graceful walk.

Murray wanted to laugh for the first time since his arrival. He managed to suppress the impulse, just as Blizzard beamed on the gathering and launched his spiel.

'Well, I bet you think this is a crazy setup. Hey?'

A nervous giggle from the girl Heather and some incomprehensible crack from Adrian.

'I suspected as much.' Blizzard's beam vanished. 'Right! As of now, you stop thinking so. This place may still look like a country club, but it isn't. It just happens to be the ideal place for our venture. How many of you have seen the theatre in the new wing? I thought you would have, Murray – you have a trouper's nose.'

'Next week: Murray Douglas in Osborne's *Entertainer*,' muttered Constant. Nobody laughed.

'Only Murray looked over the theatre so far? Jesus.' Blizzard stubbed his cigar. 'Go and take a look after this discussion, will you? You'll be impressed. Okay, let's get on.

'You all know what we're going to try and do. We're going to try out something that isn't easy, but that Manuel here has done two or three times with – do I have to say it? – the kind of success some people get once in a lifetime and die happy.'

'Jean-Paul Garrigue?' Constant murmured. He timed the words perfectly. Everyone heard them, and everyone turned to look at him.

'Constant, that isn't funny,' Adrian said in a strained voice.

'I didn't mean it to be,' Constant grunted.

Had anyone found it funny? Murray glanced around. On the thin lips of Delgado he caught the last trace of a vanishing smile. He suddenly found he was looking forward to hearing what Delgado had to say for himself.

'I'm sorry about that, Manuel,' Blizzard was saying under his breath. Delgado now pulled himself forward on his chair. From the inside pocket of his dark blue jacket he extracted a large gold cigarette case; from the case, a king-size cigarette which he lit with a gold lighter.

'Am I supposed to mind?' he said. His voice was low and his English accent good, with tantalizing traces of Argentine-Spanish and generalized United States overlaid on that. 'Make no mistake, if Jean-Paul had not already been on the edge of suicide he would not have made *Trois Fois* the – the success it became.'

Smoke wreathed from his nostrils. He cocked his head, a

little more like a reptile yet. 'You know nothing about me, any of you. There is a reputation, of course and some of you have perhaps seen a film I made. None of you have seen *Trois Fois*. If you had, you would not be here. I am uninterested in repeating myself. I am interested in one thing only. Listen and I will tell you what it is, and when I say listen I *order* you to listen because this is what you are going to live.'

It wasn't the words. It was the manner of their delivery – the fantastic conceit, the weight of meaning he managed to load on a single syllable every time he said 'I' – which took their attention.

Murray hunched forward on his chair, his scalp prickling. He had been in the presence of competence all his working life, talent more times than he could remember, and arrogant genius perhaps half a dozen times in all. Add one. This was a man with dynamite behind his eyes.

'All the time and everywhere there is one thing that we are told, and we know it is true. It is said in learned articles, in long books, in church sermons and philosophy seminars. We, are in a period of decay. Not decadence – decay. Here is a man in this age which prides itself that the individual is respected, important, unique.' The thin upper lip curled and sarcasm pointed the words. 'This man is a dummy, and inside he is foul. Do you know him? He has no goal. He is made an individual by decree, and he is soft crumbling dirt inside, and he is ashamed to want what he wants which is relief from the unceasing need to make up his own mind. He will clutch at anything – he will copy his neighbours to save making a decision of his own, he will take his neighbour's wife to bed to save mending his marriage which like a complicated machine has gone wrong and grinds and sheds metallic powder on the floor. He will have children because in them he sees some hope of rescuing a shadow of himself from the wreck of his youth, and he will drive them to wreck their youth in turn. In the end he will resort to drink' – he looked at Murray, and Murray felt like a small boy who has misbehaved in school.

'Or drugs! Or the lying consolation of religion which tells him when he dies he will be rewarded for being a creep. And he is not alone, this man. There are a thousand million of him in the world at the moment, surrounded by armour of washing-machines, shod with three-hundred-horsepower winged sandals, drowning his mind in an endless delusion of other places and other times. He is Phaëthon, so conceited he has stolen the sun's chariot. He is Andromeda's father, so proud of his daughter's beauty that the gods are made angry and compel him to chain her to a rock for a sea monster to devour, while he wrings his foolish hands and moans – "what did I do, what did I do?"' His voice slid up to a parody-falsetto on the repeated question.

'He makes me sick, and he makes you sick. Everyone knows him and nobody understands him, so nothing is done about him. *That* is what interests me, and for the next four weeks – and as long afterwards as the play runs in London or anywhere else – that is what is going to interest you. I make myself clear?'

He tapped the ash from his cigarette and leaned back, his snake's eyes darting from face to face as though inciting a challenge.

There was a long silence. Finally Ida stirred and spoke.

'Are we to take it, Mr Delgado, that the form you wish to give the result of our – our collectively developed work is that of social criticism?'

'If you mean: will it contain a plea for reform, then the answer is no.' Delgado spoke quite calmly. 'I am an artist, not a doctor. My speciality is cancer and gangrene, at the stage where the disease is past hope of cure.'

He looked at his cigarette with some distaste and stubbed it out. Then he pushed back his chair and rose.

'We will assemble for preliminary thematic discussion at nine-thirty tomorrow morning. Good night.'

5

After that, Murray wanted fresh air. He had been intending to corner Blizzard and take up the matter of the bottles he had found in his room, but the hell with it. While the others tried to pick up where they had left off on Delgado's entrance, he slipped outside. There was a stone plinth in front of the porch which was a convenient height for sitting on; he perched himself there and lit a cigarette, staring moodily at the dark forms of the bushes along the drive.

He was completely lost in his own thoughts when a voice spoke hesitantly from behind him.

'Mr Douglas? You are Murray Douglas, aren't you?'

It was Heather. He half turned, seeing her as an indistinct silhouette against the light paint of the front door, which she had closed behind her.

'Oh, hullo. Ida let you off the leash for a minute?' He hadn't meant to say anything as cutting as that – the gloomy drift of his musings dictated the words.

'I'm – sorry? I don't quite – ?'

'Never mind. Yes, I'm Murray Douglas.' He threw his spent cigarette butt into the darkness, a tiny red shooting star. 'Why?'

'I thought you were, but I wasn't sure, and I didn't like to ask anybody.' The girl gave a nervous chuckle. 'I can't quite get used to what's happened. I keep feeling I ought to be going around asking for autographs the way I used to.'

'Have half a plinth,' Murray said, shifting to one end of the cold stone on which he sat. 'Cigarette?'

'No thanks, Mr Douglas. I've been smoking too much this evening.' She moved down the last of the steps from the porch and sat beside him. With a trace of excitement colouring her voice, she went on, 'You know, I can't get over this! I remember seeing you in *Skeleton* when I was at school and thinking what a wonderful performance that was, and – here I am, so soon afterwards!'

Five years ago, Murray reminded himself. *So soon afterwards! My God!*

'What do you think of all this, Mr Douglas?' she went on after a pause. 'I've never heard of anything quite like it before – have you?'

'Stop calling me mister,' Murray said. 'I probably look old enough to be your father, but I'm not.'

A startled hiss of indrawn breath. 'I – I'm very sorry!'

Murray hesitated and finally gave a laugh. It *was* funny, in a crazy sort of way. 'Forget it. What's your name, by the way? Nobody told me.'

'Heather Carson.'

No bells. 'And how did you get mixed up in this, Heather?'

'Well – I don't really know, to be honest.' Another nervous chuckle. 'I've been in rep in Southampton for the past year, since I finished at the Gourlay School; I did two years there. I suppose I must have impressed Mr Blizzard. He came down to see us a couple of months ago, and then – well, I got this invitation.'

Of all the places Murray might have suspected, the Gourlay School was about the last he would have picked for a kid like this to have studied at. Gourlay was all Method-and-water. Well, no matter. Clearly he had also been wrong about a connexion with Ida, or she would probably have mentioned it.

She was repeating her earlier question. 'What do you make of all this – uh – Murray?'

'You really want to know?' He took out his cigarette case and lit another. 'All right, I'll tell you my impression so far. Delgado knows what he's doing. Sam Blizzard doesn't. When I was – no, it doesn't matter where I heard it. But I heard Burnett of the *Gazette* say that Sam had collected a gang of no-goods and washouts, and with the exception of yourself he's damned right. I've never seen such a collection of second standard bearers in my life.'

There was a stunned silence beside him. Finally she said, 'But I don't understand. There's yourself, to start with. I mean, you've been a star for six or seven years, haven't you?'

Murray got to his feet. 'Past tense,' he said. 'Excuse me for saying it, but I have to say it to somebody. Who do we have here? Me, since you brought the subject up – the guy who drank himself from West End leads to the line outside an agent's office in six short months. Ida Marr, who – ah, skip it. If you don't know about Ida yet, you'll find out soon enough. Adrian Gardner, too. Don't you remember Ade and the row there was about the fourteen-year-old boy he'd picked up in Oxford? He was damned lucky he didn't get jailed for that. I don't give a hoot for people's private lives provided they keep them private, but Ade can't. And then there's Gerry, Gerry

Hoading. He was a boy wonder like me, wasn't he? A few years ago people were talking about him in hushed tones, saying his work was opening a new era for the theatre the way Diaghilev's designers did for the ballet when he was hiring Picasso and God knows who. Why do you think he's here and not lounging around a Mayfair apartment saying "Sorry, too busy!" whenever the phone rings?'

'W-why?' There was a tremor in her pleasant, low-pitched voice.

Abruptly, Murray was hating himself all over again. It wasn't fair to spew out his own miserable ideas at this girl's feet. He took a deep breath.

'Skip it. I don't want to play holier-than-thou.'

'No, you mustn't leave it there. I can't tell if you're just being snide and bitter or –' She broke off, as though afraid of her own presumption.

Damn. Why did I have to start on this, anyway? Murray said tiredly, 'Okay, okay. The poor bastard is hooked. He's a junkie. Without his stuff he doesn't produce anything. With it he's so unreliable nobody can afford to take him on. He's the way I got to be when I was drinking. Satisfied?'

There was no answer. Feeling as though he had just kicked a kid's toys to pieces, he grunted a good night and went back into the house, sweating from head to toe. They were still living it up in the lounge; it sounded as though they were dancing. *Did* Delgado know what he was playing at? Or, by relying on Blizzard – who had assembled this bunch of crumbs – had he proved that he didn't? The answer eluded him. He went up to his room, to take a shower before turning in and rinse the bad feeling off his body.

It didn't work. He took another tranquillizer as well, and reflected that he was going to use up his stock of the pills pretty quickly at this rate.

Just before climbing into bed, it occurred to him to check the wardrobe and see if Valentine had carried out his instructions. He had. There was now a neat group of cans of assorted fruit juices on the shelf, and the siphon and the remaining bottles had been removed. So far, so good. He put out the light and lay down.

He had nightmares.

The gentle noise of the bedside phone brought him out of uneasy slumber in the morning. When he groped it to his ear, he heard Valentine's voice, more impersonal than ever through the frequency-cutting effect of the instrument, informing him that breakfast was served from eight until nine. He muttered thanks and swung his feet to the floor before he could lapse back to sleep.

So – now for it. He fumbled his feet into slippers, put on the robe he had left lying across the bed, and went to the washbasin. He hadn't finished his unpacking yesterday, and his shaving tackle was still in his bag. After he'd shaved, he opened the mirrored cupboard above the basin, meaning to put his razor, shaving-cream and after-shave lotion into it. There was a tooth mug in the cupboard. There was also a half-bottle of Scotch.

He stared at it for an eternal moment, incredulously. Then a wave of rage darkened his mind. He caught the bottle from the shelf, snapped the neck against the side of the wash-basin, and let the contents flood down the drain. The smell sickened him; after a moment, he dropped the bottle and went across the room to the phone. There was no dial on it. He picked it up and waited.

Shortly, he heard Valentine. 'Yes, Mr Douglas? What can I do for you?'

'Why the hell was there a bottle of whisky in the medicine cabinet in my room?'

'A bottle of whisky, sir? I'm very surprised to hear that.'

'Are you? Are you really?' Murray drew a deep breath. 'Well, get this. If I find any more liquor in this room, I shall bring it to you and force it down your throat, and I will push the bottle after it. Do you understand? Now get someone up here to clear away the mess!'

'I will attend to it myself when breakfast is over, Mr Douglas. Ah – perhaps I should remind you that it is now twenty-five minutes past eight o'clock.'

'Oh, go to hell!' Murray said and slammed the phone down. He looked around the room, clenching his fists. There were drawers aplenty, the shelves of the wardrobe, the bookcase, the shoe-rack. There was the bed. He remembered very well that in places such as those he had once hidden his own liquor from friends and doctors.

He made a minute check. Finding nothing, he began to relax. He felt a pang of appetite accompanying his relief, and realized that there had been a point to Valentine's remark about the time. He started to dress.

Most of his clothes were still in his bag and would now have to stay there until later. He went to get out a favourite sweater, which had been packed first and was consequently at the bottom, and underneath it he found another bottle of whisky.

He seized it by the neck, unwilling to believe that it was real until he could feel it cool and solid to the touch, and a whisper of terror went across his mind like a bitter winter wind. This was a twin of the bottle in the medicine cabinet. Had he himself –?

No, by God, I didn't. And I'm going to take Sam Blizzard by the neck as I've got this bottle and make him tell me what devil's trick he's playing!

He swung around and hurled the bottle fair at the wall over the washbasin. Splinters of glass flew, and there was a vast brown splash as the whisky poured after what had already gone down the drain.

He pulled on the sweater and made for the door.

All right, Blizzard, damn you. Here I come.

6

But Blizzard wasn't in the dining room. There were two young men he knew by sight sitting together at the far end of the long table, but everyone else appeared to have finished except Heather, who sat by herself near the door. There was an unused place-setting next to her. Murray hooked out the chair from it and sat down, and the black-suited man waiting by the sideboard picked up a glass of orange juice to place before him.

'Morning,' Murray said. 'Seen Blizzard?'

'Oh – oh, good morning, Murray.' She had been preoccupied and only now noticed who had joined her. 'I was – uh – going to keep that place for Ida. She asked me.'

She would. 'Skin Ida,' Murray said. 'Have you seen Blizzard?'

'Well . . . Yes, he's already finished breakfast. Went out a few minutes ago.' She hesitated. 'Is something wrong?'

'Yes. Never mind, it's nothing to do with you.' He gulped down the orange juice, and for a moment in his imagination it filled his nose and throat with the hotness of whisky. He put the glass down and said under his breath, 'God *damn*.'

'Well, well! Morning, Murray!' With acid sweetness, Ida's voice came from behind him. 'Is that the place you were going to keep for me, Heather darling?'

'I'm sorry, Ida. I didn't have a chance to –'

'Oh, never mind. There's one opposite, I see.' On stage as ever, Ida swept around the end of the table. She had put on black jeans and a black sweater and wound her throat with a chain of enormous gilded links. She looked tired. 'My own fault for being late, I guess. Thank you' – to the bringer of orange juice. 'I'll just have some dry toast after this, and about a gallon of black coffee. What's up with you, Murray? Hangover?'

The glass before Murray was deftly exchanged for a plate of cornflakes. He picked up his spoon and didn't say anything.

'Not funny?' Ida said brightly. 'Never mind, Murray, you'll be over it by lunchtime.'

'Stow it,' Murray said. 'I'm on the wagon and you know it.'

'So you were telling us last night. That's why I thought it was so peculiar when I passed your room just now. The door was open and one of these vampiric valets they keep here was clearing up some kind of mess. And there was a stink of Scotch you could cut with a knife.'

She smiled with honey and venom. At his side, Murray was aware of Heather looking at him, horrified. His desire for food vanished like a flame blown out.

'This place isn't a country club,' he said, pushing back his chair. 'It's a lunatic asylum. Or if we go on like this for four solid weeks we're going to turn it into one. Don't let me interfere with your new romance, will you, Ida?' he ended savagely as he spun on his heel.

She deserved that for the crack about a hangover. But I wish Heather didn't have to be there and hear me.

Nine-thirty, and astonishingly everyone was present, on time, in the miniature theatre – except, once again, for Delgado and Blizzard. Last of the other arrivals was Lester Harkham, the lean, fortyish lighting expert who almost always worked on Blizzard's productions. He came from backstage when the rest had settled down, jumped to the auditorium floor, and, before dropping into a seat next to Gerry Hoading, announced that Delgado and Blizzard would be with them in a few minutes.

Murray looked around. There was a piano with an electronic keyboard at one side of the stage, and Jess Aumen was sitting on its stool, moving one hand idly over the keys but not making them sound. He was a sleek young man with the artificially polished good looks of a male model, but he was a good composer, undoubtedly.

Lester, Jess, Blizzard himself and Gerry if he could be kept on the rails: that was as good a supporting team as you could hope for. Then why in heaven's name hadn't he lined up more talent to put on stage? Apart from those with whom Murray had worked before, there were only the two young men who had been finishing breakfast when he arrived – Rett Latham and Al Wilkinson – and a girl called Cherry Bell, about whom he knew nothing. She was sitting with Rett and Al in the front row.

People were tensed up. You could feel it without following their conversation.

Then Blizzard and Delgado appeared from backstage, Blizzard carrying one chair and dragging another which made scraping and bumping sounds on the floor. He set them facing the others over the footlights, and he and Delgado sat down.

The author took out, with theatrical deliberation, another of his king-size cigarettes and lit it with a flourish. Today he had put on a sharkskin jacket and fawn trousers, and there was a pearl the size of a pellet of buckshot on his tie.

'Okay, let's get on,' Blizzard said after a general nod to his listeners. 'First –'

'First, Sam!' Murray hauled himself to his feet and planted both hands, palm down, on the back of the seat before him. 'I'd have raised this with you privately, but you've been generating your aura of mystery and busy-ness, and I've not been able to get at you. I want you to tell me why the devil you've been telling your slimy creature Valentine to scatter bottles of liquor all over my room.'

There was an endless-seeming silence. During it, Delgado's calculating dark eyes fixed on Murray and stayed there. An expression of interest developed very slowly around those eyes, like an image appearing on a photographic film.

'You must be crazy, Murray,' Blizzard said at length. 'I know damned well why you're on the wagon, and I wouldn't do anything to push you off. I suppose what you mean is that I told Valentine to leave some drinks in everybody's rooms and forgot to warn him to skip yours. I did forget to tell him. I'm sorry and it won't happen again.'

'Not good enough, Sam.' Murray hunched forward. 'There were bottles left openly on a shelf along with glasses and some soda, and that's okay – I had those taken out. But I want to know why another bottle was put in the medicine cabinet and another hidden at the bottom of my travelling bag.'

There was another silence. Delgado raised a finely drawn eyebrow, and Murray could hear the tumblers clicking in Blizzard's mind. The director scowled at length.

'I don't know anything about them, Murray. And I think it would be a damned good idea if you shut up and sit down before I tell you the only way I can think of for a bottle to get into your bag.'

Murray looked around him. Everyone else was regarding him steadily. Ida Marr was smiling a little, but the others were sullen or worried. He hesitated, calling himself every kind of a damned fool for not waiting till he could get Blizzard alone.

'No, don't sit down, Douglas!'

The words came softly from Delgado. The author had stirred and was leaning forward with a speculative expression now. 'You begin to be interesting. You suggest a theme. A persecution. If I understand, you are saying that someone is attempting to make you drink again when you are forbidden to.'

'I'm saying nothing of the sort,' Murray snapped, and dropped back into his seat.

'Now consider this.' As though the denial hadn't been spoken, Delgado took a large pad of paper and a pen from the side pocket of his jacket, and poised it to make notes. 'Cherry, come up here.'

The girl about whom Murray knew nothing obeyed. She moved to the edge of the stage near Delgado's feet, turned around and hoisted herself up with legs swinging. She put a shorthand pad on her knee, produced a pen of her own, and slipped a pair of horn-rimmed glasses on.

Oh. Murray had assumed she was a member of the cast. But you would need someone to fix the suggestions as they were made and to type up draft scripts; that must be her assignment.

'Consider forms of persecution,' Delgado was saying. 'By advertisement, for instance – you don't have a particular gewgaw, you're a slob.'

'Chasing people who already have serviceable objects to replace them with flashy new ones,' Constant put in. 'That's a kind of persecution, if you're looking at it your way.'

'Right. More?'

It grew. It grew incredibly. By lunchtime it had taken such a grip on them that they barely dragged themselves away to the dining room. Even Murray was forced out of his angry withdrawal, and the air began to smell of electricity. By afternoon they had stepped through half a scene, about forty extemporized exchanges that served to delineate a pair of characters, and Jess Aumen was improvising angular modern chords. Also improvising, in his own way, was Gerry Hoading. He had clearly got his supply of dope from somewhere; his face was flushed and his voice kept sliding up the scale towards shrillness. But his imagination was working double time, and before they stepped through the brief action he chalked out the stage for them and laid out with gestures an entire two-level set which in itself implied further possibilities of action.

At five o'clock Delgado abruptly stopped everything, told Cherry to go away and type up her notes, and taking Blizzard's arm, disappeared backstage. The tension dropped but didn't disappear; the effect was that of a punctured tyre with a safety reserve cushioning the collapse.

They drifted back to the lounge, arguing at the tops of their voices, and the arguments went on all evening.

It was a long, long time since Murray had seen enthusiasm of this order generated so quickly. And it was due to Delgado, no one else. The mind was keen and darting; even though he was working in a foreign language his ear was sharp enough to catch and correct the least infelicity in a proposed line, and his corrections were so transparently right that not even Ida had tried to contradict him.

How long would it last? They were going to work again tomorrow. By this time next week, Murray judged, tiredness would be competing with enthusiasm. But then they might have a complete outline, and presumably it would take Delgado a couple of days to organize and edit his script. Oh, it was beginning to look feasible.

Tonight, nobody had the bad taste to try and make him take a drink, so that was all right. When the talk lost its intensity and one or two people – Heather, Jess Aumen – had drifted to bed, he decided he'd better do the same.

Getting up, he tossed a casual good night to the others and made for the door. Behind him, someone else rose, and in the hallway he heard his name called. He turned back. Gerry Hoading was coming out of the lounge.

'Murray, mind if I have a private word with you?'

'No, surely – go ahead.'

'Let's keep walking. I'm turning in, too.' Gerry waved towards the winding stairs. 'Uh – I don't quite know how to put this, but I've got to say it. Look, you know my trouble, don't you? We've worked together before, so I guess you must.'

'Yes, I know about it. Why?'

The young designer put his hands together, twisted them so that the knuckles cracked and let them fall to his sides. 'Well, I – I have enough of the stuff to keep me going. I don't know where the hell Sam got it from, but I found it in my room when I got here, the way you found the liquor you were talking about this morning, and I wasn't complaining. I've been taken off the stuff once, and it nearly killed me, and it certainly was going to kill me professionally, so I'm stuck with it.'

He was sweating, and his low voice shook a little. They reached the head of the stairs and turned back into the new wing.

'This is my room – number ten,' he went on, stopping and fishing for a key. 'I figure I must be just about over the middle row of seats in the theatre. Crazy thing to find, isn't it? A private theatre equipped like that! No, come in, Murray, I haven't finished.'

He stood aside and gestured for Murray to go in. The room was very much like Murray's, apart from the colour of the bedcover and curtains.

'Look, what I'm trying to say is this.' Gerry shut the door and stood twisting the key between his hands. 'You must have some kind of guts that I don't have. I hardly even have the guts to ask you what I am going to ask. But I know I've got to, if you follow me. Here!'

He spun on his heel and pulled out a drawer from a chest under the window; from the drawer he produced a two-ounce jar almost full of fine white dust.

'I've never seen so much of it in my life at one time,' he almost whispered. 'A thousand pounds' worth? Heaven knows how much it must have cost! Because it isn't cut, you see – it's simon-pure heroin. And if I – well, when things – oh, God *damn*! Murray, will you take charge of it for me? Right now I have enough self-control to ask you, but I may not pluck up the courage again. Things have gone damned well today. Too well, maybe. I don't know. If they turn sour, I know from experience that I won't have the patience to load myself and wait for the stuff to hit. I'll go crazy waiting and take on a second load, and I'll probably make it a bigger one, if I have this much of the stuff ready to hand. And when I do that I'll kill myself. I know perfectly well I will. Here!'

He thrust the jar towards Murray as though terrified he might change his mind in the next minute. 'Keep it for me, will you? Don't tell me where you're hiding it. Lock it up if you can. Never let me take more than three grains at one go, have you got that? Not even if something goes wildly wrong, and the project looks like breaking down, and I come *crying* to you for more, don't for God's sake let me take more than three grains!'

Murray nodded, hefted the little jar in his hand and turned towards the door. As he reached for the handle, Gerry spoke again.

'Murray, I – I'm very grateful for this. I haven't any right to ask you to do this for me. If there's anything I can do in return, just let me know, won't you?'

'Sure,' Murray muttered and went out.

7

Murray put on the light in his own room, closed the door, and looked around him ruefully.

God, was there ever such a spavined, windbroken, knock-kneed string put together as this bunch here?

But at least the experience of the first day's work with Delgado had improved Gerry Hoading. From their previous acquaintance, Murray wouldn't have credited him with the self-control necessary to separate himself from his precious drug.

Now – where to hide the stuff? A drawer or cupboard was much too obvious. Outside on a window sill? He peered through the darkness of the glass between the drawn curtains. No joy – the sill was only a lip, half an inch wide. Inside the back of the TV set, then. That had been one of his own most successful inspirations when he was hiding his liquor.

This was a modern slim-line set, though. When he turned it around and peered through the ventilation slits in the back, he couldn't see any space large enough to accept the bottle he held without interfering with the circuitry. Besides, the back of the set was fixed with some special kind of fastening, not ordinary screws which he could have removed with his pocket-knife. He bit his lip and put the set the way it had been.

He considered his travelling bag, but when he checked his

key ring he found the bag's key wasn't on it. Since he hadn't locked the bag on leaving home, he hadn't noticed the missing key before. The hell. Gerry's stuff would just have to go under the mattress for the time being. Maybe a better place would turn up later.

He pulled back the bedding accordingly. As he did so, his foot knocked against the base of the bed – which in fact was a divan rather than a bed, with a box base and only a couple of inches clearance from the floor. The noise his shoe made rang hollow, but he didn't realize the significance of the fact immediately.

Under the bottom sheet, the mattress. And embroidered on it a curiously complex design in metallic thread, running almost the full width of the mattress and about eighteen inches in depth – approximately, in fact, the area over which the bolster would lie.

Curious. Never seen a mattress like that before.

But he gathered a fistful of the ticking and lifted the head of the mattress with a grunt. Then he saw why the side of the bed had sounded hollow when his foot struck it.

There was a hinged panel cut into the base.

What the –?

With considerable straining, he managed to get the mattress off entirely and let it slide to the floor with the bedding tangled around it. Something went *twang* as he did this, and a glint caught his eye. Moving his head, he lost it again. He put out a cautious hand and located a metal thread as fine as gossamer running from the embroidered pattern on the mattress into the side of the hinged panel. The fall of the mattress had stretched it taut and then broken it. When he pulled at it experimentally, it felt as sharp as a razor.

He put his fingernails under the edge of the hinged panel and opened it.

Below, he found a tape deck. At first glance, it looked quite ordinary. It wasn't switched on. There were two enormous – professional-size – spools of conventional oxide-coated tape; about a third of it had wound from the left-hand spool to the right. A second glance revealed that there were no controls on the deck – just the spool turrets and the heads.

Murray studied it for a while and then shrugged. No good kidding himself; he knew from nothing about tape recorders except to switch them on or off. He very much wanted to know, though, what the hell a tape recorder was doing in the head of his bed. Was this another of the country club's facilities? Soothing music under the pillow to lull the members to sleep? All right. Then where was the speaker, and how did you turn the music off if you wanted to?

He straightened with a frown. He wasn't going to be able to put his head down on this bed before he'd asked a few pertinent questions. He picked up Gerry's bottle from the bedside where he'd left it while wrestling with the mattress. Blazes! He still had to find somewhere to hide it, and he'd better do that before leaving.

A possibility occurred to him. There was a pelmet along the curtain rail. It might just be roomy enough to take the bottle on its side, resting on the rail. It was. He drew the curtains back and forth a couple of times to make sure he wouldn't dislodge the bottle; satisfied, he left it there and went out.

At the same moment, Gerry emerged from the toilet at the far end of the corridor and started back to his room. He gave a sickly grin on seeing Murray and muttered a good night.

'Gerry, just a moment,' Murray said, striding towards him. 'Mind if I check up on something?'

'Uh – sure. What?' Gerry blinked at him.

'Let me look at your bed, will you? I want to see if mine is a special case, or whether all the beds have them.'

'Have what?' Bewildered, Gerry watched as Murray peeled back his bedding and revealed first the metal-thread embroidery on the mattress, then an identical hinged panel opening above an identical tape-deck. Perhaps slightly less of the tape had wound on to the take-up spool of this one.

'Good grief,' Gerry said blankly. 'What's that for?'

'I haven't got the slightest idea,' Murray answered. 'But I'd like to know, I must say.'

'I suppose you found yours while hiding my – my stuff.' Gerry gave a weak chuckle. 'Well, that's one place I needn't bother to look, anyway.'

'That's right.' Murray felt for the strong fine metal thread linking the mattress with the bed's base, which he had been careful not to snap. This time he traced it all the way to the corner of the tape-deck; it disappeared there down a tiny metal tube.

'Do you imagine it's lullaby music for the people who used to come here when it was a country club?' Gerry ventured. 'A pretty sybaritic place, it must have been – I wouldn't put an idea like that past whoever designed it.'

'I thought of that myself,' Murray nodded. 'Trouble is, I can't see any sign of a speaker down here.' He was peering into the cavity holding the tape-deck.

'You'd expect the speaker to be on top of the mattress, not under it,' Gerry suggested, poking with interest at the metal-thread embroidery.

There was an exclamation from Murray. Gerry swung around. 'What's wrong?' he demanded.

'What did you do just then?' Murray countered. 'Do it again, whatever it was.'

'I was only touching this embroidery here,' Gerry said. He put out his hand again. 'I was –'

'That's it,' Murray cut in. 'I see; you're pressing on part of the embroidered pattern. So there's a switch somewhere. Look, the tape's running.'

At the full reach of his arm, Gerry craned to see. Sure enough, the turrets were turning steadily.

'Well, where's your music?' Murray asked.

Gerry glanced at him and then back at the slowly unreeling tape. 'It is odd, isn't it? Uh – do you suppose the tape's been wiped by accident?'

'It might have. Look, don't strain yourself! You can stop pressing on the mattress now.' Murray dusted his hands together. 'So we'll have to eliminate that possibility, too. Do you know which is Lester Harkham's room? I imagine he's the only person here who knows anything about electronics.'

'No. No, I don't know which is his room.' Gerry licked his lips. 'Murray, aren't you making rather a big thing out of this? Surely it doesn't make any odds one way or the other. Suppose you do find one which plays music – so what? Why can't you go back and see if yours does, come to that?'

'Because I broke the thread linking the mattress with the base.' Murray looked thoughtfully at the embroidery on the mattress, then touched it. 'Only takes quite a light contact to start the spools turning, you notice. It's probably meant to respond to the weight of your head on the pillow.'

There was a faint sound of footsteps from the corridor; a door opened and closed.

'There's somebody now,' Murray said. 'Come on.'

A little puzzled, Gerry shrugged and complied.

Out in the corridor, however, it proved impossible to tell which room the owner of the footsteps had entered. Murray sighed. He put his ear to number eleven, the one next to Gerry's, then to twelve, and after each shook his head.

'There's nobody in thirteen,' Gerry said with a forced chuckle. 'I asked Valentine.'

'And fourteen's mine. Must be the other end, then. Let's try nine.' Murray went back. Beyond the door of number nine he caught a faint sound of conversation and knocked.

'Who is it?'

Why Heather. How interesting. Murray laid a small bet with himself. Aloud, he said, 'Murray here. Gerry Hoading's with me. Can we come in? It's rather important.'

A whispered exchange which Murray didn't follow; then: 'All right, come in. The door's open.'

He turned the handle. Heather was sitting up in bed, her face very pink and young without makeup, a satin bed jacket over her black nightgown. On a chair beside the bed was Ida, still in her rehearsal outfit; she had a cigarette in one hand and a glass in the other – a martini, by the look of it. Murray paid out on his bet.

'Well!' Ida drawled as Murray shut the door after letting Gerry pass him. 'To what do we owe this honour, friends?'

'Heather, do something for me, will you?' Murray said. 'Lean on your pillow – hard – and listen to it. Is there music coming from it when you do that?'

'What on earth –?' Heather began. Then she gave a giggle and did as she was asked, with elaborate pantomime of putting her ear to the ground. Straightening again, she shook her head.

'All right, what's the punch line?' Ida demanded.

'None so far,' Murray snapped. 'But if you'll hop out of bed, Heather, I'll show you why I asked.'

Uncertainly, she looked from him to Ida and back again.

'There's some kind of gadget hidden in the bases of these beds,' Gerry said. 'Murray's getting a thing about them, and he won't let anyone rest till he's solved his mystery.'

'What sort of gadget?' Heather said, bewildered. 'Oh – very well. Ida darling, give me my dressing gown, will you? Over the back of your chair.'

She got deftly out from between the sheets with decorum to satisfy the Lord Chamberlain, and Murray proceeded to show what he was talking about – the embroidery, the connecting metal thread, and the tape-deck hidden in the base.

Even Ida was startled out of her cynical manner when she saw what was revealed. 'I see what you mean about music coming from the pillow,' she admitted. 'But there's nothing happening at the moment, is there? The spools just go around when you lean on the mattress.' She pressed the mattress herself to prove the point.

It occurred to Murray that there was a condition in which a tape recorder never made a noise of its own: when it was recording, not playing back. In this connexion, the point seemed irrelevant. He had no idea why it should make his skin crawl for a moment.

'Any idea where I can find Sam Blizzard?' he asked. 'As Gerry said, I'm not likely to sleep until I've got to the bottom of this.'

Ida laughed. 'You're a screwball, Murray. So long as the one in my bed is as quiet as this one I imagine I'll sleep fine!' She turned to stub her cigarette and emptied her glass with a quick gesture. 'But if you really want to beard Sam in his den, then I think you'll find him and Delgado having a *tête-à-tête* in the room on the right of the dining room. They're using that as an office, sort of – they have the typewriter in there and the duplicator for scripts. Me, I'm going to call it a day. 'Night, Heather honey.'

She bestowed smiles all round and went out. After a pause, Gerry spread his hands and did the same.

'Murray, I wish you hadn't made me know about this thing in

the bed,' Heather said, staring down at the tape-deck. 'It's absurd, but it makes me feel creepy – it being there, and no obvious reason for it. *Is* there a reason?'

'I don't know, darling,' Murray said grimly. 'But I'm going right to Sam to find out, and if I do I'll come back and let you know. Okay?'

8

Without knocking, he tried the handle of the door on the right of the dining room to which Ida had directed him. It was locked. Beyond, he could hear the purr of an electric typewriter and a mutter of voices, which stopped as the noise of the turning handle came to the speakers.

'Just a moment,' Blizzard said. Murray drew back from the door. Shortly there was a click and it was opened by Blizzard.

'Oh, it's you, Murray. What do you want?'

'Do I have to talk through the door, or can I come in?'

Blizzard hesitated, then shrugged and drew back. Murray went past him. This room would have been the secretary's office in the country club, perhaps; there was a big desk, a pair of matched file cabinets, an electric duplicator. At a table against the wall the girl Cherry Bell sat, her fingers flying over the keys of the typewriter he had already heard. In an easy chair, Delgado was turning typed pages on his knee; marking his place with a finger, he looked up interestedly on Murray's entrance.

'Well?' Blizzard pressed him. 'Is it something important, Murray? It's getting very late, and we haven't finished working through today's material yet.'

'It's about the tape recorders hidden in our beds,' Murray said. He spoke to Blizzard, but his eyes were on Delgado, and he was obscurely delighted to see an expression of dismay and even alarm fleet over that beautifully controlled visage.

'What on earth are you talking about?' Blizzard said. 'Really, Murray! What kind of state are you in? If this is like the row you tried to kick up this morning, then I can see I'm going to lose patience with you pretty quickly.'

'Ask Delgado if it's nonsense,' Murray said, still staring at the writer. 'He knows what I mean. Don't you, Delgado?'

'Yes. Yes, I know.' Delgado shifted easily on his chair and put his pile of papers on the corner of Cherry's typing table. 'It's part of my method of working, about which so far you've learned practically nothing. Those tape recorders have fitted in very conveniently.'

Murray had an indefinable feeling that Delgado was improvising his answer, but there was nothing to prove it.

'Go on,' he challenged harshly.

'Do you understand the meaning of the word hypnopaedia?'

There was a pause. Murray glanced at Blizzard and saw that the portly director was as much in the dark as he himself.

Very illuminating, he glossed with sarcasm. Aloud, he said, 'You mean this notion which keeps cropping up about getting a higher education painlessly in your sleep? I've heard of it. And I'm also aware that it doesn't work.'

'Have it your way.' Delgado made a graceful gesture of dismissal with one hand. 'For me, it works excellently. I always employ it. I am not satisfied with a cast which puts on a rôle for a few hours in the theatre and for the remainder of the day reverts to totally different behaviour. I require a depth of identification which not even the Method provides. Hypnopaedia offers a technique for achieving this. That's all.'

'Manuel, I'm not quite clear what you're talking about,' Blizzard put in.

'Aren't you?' Murray said. 'Then listen. At the head of my bed, and Gerry Hoading's, and Heather's, there are hidden tape-decks. These are connected to some kind of switch in the mattress; when you lie down, the tape begins to run. Delgado is trying to say that these are for perfecting a rôle during sleep – that you get your lines or something repeated and repeated to you. What lines are you thinking of giving to Gerry Hoading, Delgado? He's a designer, not an actor.'

Was that a trace of sweat shiny on the author's sallow forehead? Murray couldn't be sure.

'Murray, you are making a great fuss, aren't you?' Delgado

countered. 'I didn't install these recorders specially, you know. They were intended to play soothing music if required by the users of the country club. They are in all the beds.'

'Really! There are two things wrong with this explanation: first, there's no sign of a speaker with any of them – and second, the tapes, which are still in place, are apparently blank.'

'Oh, *dear*.' Delgado made the trite phrase bear a weight of exaggerated patience. 'Murray, these instruments have not been used for some while. I have had them reconnected so that it can be established whether they are all properly operating. You can't do this without putting a spool of tape on each of them – which I have had done. Of course the tape is blank! As for the speakers which you didn't find: they are inside the mattress. Moreover, even when instruction tapes are used, you will not hear them consciously. The sound is at the very limit of audible perception. It is in fact subliminal. If it were louder it would risk disturbing the sleeper and ruining the value of the technique. Now I hope you're satisfied. And I also hope – Sam! – that you will be able to persuade Murray not to fly off the handle at any other unusual aspects of my personal method of working.'

Blizzard took a cigar from the front pocket of his jacket and mechanically bit the end. He said, 'Why didn't you mention this to me, Manuel? It's an interesting idea, but I'm not sure I –'

'You will see its effectiveness soon enough, Sam,' Delgado cut in. 'The only reason I hadn't mentioned it was because the existence of tape-decks hidden in the beds meant I did not have to ask you for a special supply of recorders. But for that, you would have had to hire me a dozen of them, and I would have explained why. Is this really worth so much fuss?'

'I guess not.' Blizzard looked at his cigar as though wondering what it was doing in his hand. 'But if you have any more surprises like this to spring on the cast, Manuel, it might be better to warn them in advance.'

'No. Positively not.' Delgado gave an emphatic head-shake. 'As it is, I am a little annoyed that Murray has stumbled on this. There may be a tendency to resist subconsciously the educational effect of the tape. However, we shall see.

Perhaps when you have some experience of the value of hypnopaedia, Murray, you will accept it more readily.'

A few moments earlier, Cherry had removed the last sheets of paper from her typewriter; now she switched it off, and the room was suddenly very quiet.

'Finished, Mr Blizzard,' she said into the pause following Delgado's remark.

'Oh, good girl.' Blizzard seemed to pull himself together. 'Okay, give the last page to Mr Delgado, and you can turn in. Was that all you wanted, Murray?'

'No. Not by a long chalk. But I guess it'll have to do for now.'

In accordance with his promise, he knocked on Heather's door to tell her what Delgado had said, but got no answer; she must have dropped off to sleep. He went to his own room with his face set in such a frown he felt it threatened to become a fixture, and before putting the bed back together he traced the broken thread of metal linking the tape-deck to the mattress, wrapped it around his fingers with a handkerchief to protect his skin and pulled it free. When he was done, he had unravelled a good twenty yards of very fine wire from the embroidered area on the mattress.

Which left nothing. There was no point of attachment. There was no speaker inside the mattress. Delgado was lying.

What the devil could be the purpose of a tape-deck with no speaker? What could it be recording, since, obviously, it couldn't be playing anything back? And how? There was no microphone either. Just the wire.

Could the wire form a sort of mike, or speaker, by itself? This was the only possibility that occurred to him. He had vague impressions of new advances in printed circuitry at the back of his memory, but he had no way of telling whether a simple wire could generate or receive sound . . .

The hell with it. He turned the mattress end for end as a kind of defiance, put the bed roughly back together, and climbed in. He lay for a long time in darkness, wondering what he had let himself in for. Eventually sleep came, like a switch being turned.

Next day, he had no immediate chance to carry out his half-formed intention of questioning Lester Harkham about these tape-decks, for none of the other three who knew of them was particularly concerned, and they were as eager as the rest to get back to work. Heather did ask him what he had learned, but seemed barely interested; it was enough that Delgado had given some kind of explanation, and the point – immensely significant to Murray – that it could not have been the whole truth she dismissed with a shrug.

By the evening, Murray was coming around to the same view. Under Delgado's skilful and precise guidance, some form was already emerging from the half-baked chaos of rival ideas which had been thrown up. No doubt about it. This man was *good*.

It was so long since Murray had been caught up in the fever of a production which, from the start, everyone knew was going to be brilliant, that he had almost forgotten the sensation. Late in the afternoon he realized what was happening to him, and the shock was so great he felt weakened by it. Who the hell cared how Delgado chose to get his results? Let him use black magic if he wanted to; let him tell all the lies and half-truths he wished. You couldn't set a price on a gift such as his. It was fairly clear that no one liked him, but it was certain that he was generating immense respect.

And yet . . .

As he had done yesterday, Delgado stopped everything with a curt word at five o'clock and went backstage with Blizzard, and also as yesterday there was a sudden drop in the level of tension. They looked around as if startled to discover themselves back in the little theatre instead of their artificial world; then they began to disperse, declaring extreme exhaustion and the desperate need of a drink.

Apart from the cast, Jess Aumen stayed at his piano, experimenting with a curious harmonic progression which he could not quite get right; Gerry jumped up on the stage and walked around speculatively, a pad of paper in one hand and a steel tape in the other, making notes for his proposed set, and Lester Harkham – who had been working with the compact but remarkably extensive lighting system, playing it like a musical instrument – remained for a few moments in the aisle at the side of the little auditorium, his expression thoughtful.

Murray made up his mind and went over.

'Lester, can you spare me a few minutes?'

'Hm?' Lester seemed to come back from a great distance. 'Oh, surely, Murray. What is it?'

'Well . . .' Now it had come to the point, it did feel absurd to make such a fuss about Delgado and his tape recorders. Murray changed his line of attack smoothly. 'Look, Lester, keep this to yourself, will you? Gerry has asked me to look after a jar of horse for him, because he's afraid if he gets depressed he may overdose himself. The best place I've ever found to hide something like that is inside a TV set – he'll never think of looking there. But I can't get the back off the one in my room, and I don't want to foul up the machinery. Do you think you could give me a hand?'

For a moment Lester looked blank. 'That's about the oddest request I've ever had!' he exclaimed.

'I'm not surprised,' Murray agreed. 'I wouldn't ask you, but you're the only person here who knows anything about electronics as far as I know.'

'Well, I can find my way around a TV set okay. Sure, I'll be with you in a moment. Just let me have a word with Gerry.'

'For Christ's sake keep this to yourself, Lester! He made me promise not to –'

'All right, all right! I'm not so big a fool. Hang on. Hey, Gerry! Word with you!' Lester strode towards the stage.

So far, so good, Murray reflected. Now he could bring up the matter of the tape recorders casually. And he was looking forward with some eagerness to hearing what Lester's reaction might be to hypnopaedia and the rest of Delgado's spiel.

9

'Oh yes. Got those fancy don't-do-it-yourself fastenings on the back, I see.' Lester bent to inspect the TV set, fishing in his hip pocket. He found what he was after – a multi-purpose electrician's screwdriver – and set to work. 'What do you make of this affair so far, Murray? Bit of a phenomenon, our friend Delgado, isn't he?'

'I can't deny that I'm impressed,' Murray admitted, sitting on the edge of the bed to watch. 'Though there's a lot more I want to know about him.'

'Don't we all! Chiefly where the hell has he been hiding himself?' Lester twisted the first of the fastenings loose and attacked the next one. 'You know, when Sam Blizzard first put the plan up to me, I told him he was off his nut. Whoever heard of sinking this kind of money into this indefinite a project? He'll have spent a good five thousand just on trimmings before we leave. But now I'm beginning to think he wasn't so stupid. Take me, for instance. Normally I'd just be sitting in the back row chewing my nails. As it is, I can go up to the lighting booth and start thinking, even though there's not much more than half a scene worked out. I mean, I know what I'm doing is going to be definitive, apart from changes which Gerry may want for – *Jesus* God!'

He snatched his hand away from the TV set and let his screwdriver fall tinkling on the table where it rested. Murray jumped to his feet.

'What the devil happened?'

'This damned thing's live. I got the healthiest shock I've had in years.' Breathing hard and shaking his hand up and down, Lester bent to inspect the on-off knob. 'It says *off*, all right,' he muttered. 'Bloody thing must be faulty. But I don't see how . . .'

He went off into a string of technicalities about live chassis and condensers not discharging properly, which Murray didn't attempt to follow.

'Want me to unplug it?' he demanded.

'Yes, for heaven's sake! I ought to have done it myself.' Lester put his hand on the top of the set, then sniffed at the ventilation slots behind. 'Funny. It's stone cold, and if there were current passing you'd expect it to smell warm, at least.'

Murray closed on the thick rubber-cased cable leading from the set to the floor. It vanished at the edge of the fitted carpet; he dropped on one knee and turned the carpet back.

'Curiouser and curiouser,' he murmured. 'Lester, this flex

doesn't plug into a socket. It just goes under the skirting board. Look here.'

'Huh?' Lester came over and leaned a hand on his shoulder. 'Why, how extraordinary.'

The thick black cable ran straight to the floor. Close to the wall, a piece of one of the floorboards had been cut away, and the cable led down through the slot so created.

'That's new,' Murray said. 'Isn't it? Look, the edge of the wood is clean and white.' He moved the cable so Lester could see.

'It must be a rediffusion system,' Lester said with half-hearted optimism. 'But you usually have an external selector with rediffusion, and sound as well as the TV channels. Let me take another look at the set, if I can manage it without getting shocked again.'

Murray turned around and sat on the floor with his back to the wall. He only had to wait a short while before Lester removed the rear panel of the set, carefully placed it on the floor, and peered inside. He gave a whistle.

'Something else funny?' Murray suggested, in a tone that implied he was altogether unsurprised.

'Very funny indeed,' Lester confirmed. 'I've never seen a clutter of circuits like this in a TV set before. The basic circuitry's in here – I think – but there's a gang of other stuff been added. Murray, you didn't know about this, did you?' he interrupted himself. 'Was that story about trying to hide Gerry's horse just an excuse to have me investigate?'

'Now why should you think that?' Murray countered, genuinely startled.

'Something Ida was saying over lunch. Something about you finding weird electronic circuits in your bed.'

'Oh, I see.' Murray didn't try to hide his relief. 'I'm glad you've heard about that from someone else already.'

He ran quickly over the events of last night. While listening, Lester continued to peer around the interior of the TV set, not touching anything except a wire, which he occasionally pushed aside with the end of his screwdriver.

'And he said it was all for sleep learning, did he?' he commented when Murray had finished. 'Well, that's a lot of garbage for a start. This sleep-learning notion keeps turning up – Huxley had it in *Brave New World*, remember? – but as far as I know it's never amounted to anything. Still, I suppose if Delgado likes to kid himself that it's useful, it won't do any harm.'

'Without a speaker for the sound? I told you – I pulled all the wire off my mattress, and it came loose. There was nowhere it could have been connected to a speaker or a mike.'

'Well, there are some experimental installations –' Lester checked himself. 'No, it's ridiculous. They cost about five hundred apiece, and you wouldn't find them lying around in the bedrooms here. Can I have a look at this gadget?'

'What's left of it,' Murray said, rising. 'If Delgado was telling the truth when he said they're in all the rooms, you can see this wire embroidery on your own mattress, I imagine. But the rest of it –'

He broke off. He had turned down the bedding to reveal the mattress, and the embroidery was back.

'Delgado must take this pretty seriously,' he said. 'He's had a replacement supplied for me.' He kept his tone light, but he was taut with unaccountable alarm. 'Okay, what do you make of it?'

Lester said nothing for some moments. Then he heaved up the mattress, tracing the gossamer-fine wire to the hinged panel, and satisfied himself about the operation of the tape-deck. At length he let the mattress drop into place again.

'Tell you one thing,' he said harshly. 'This stuff on the mattress – it couldn't possibly act as either a speaker or a mike.'

'Then what's it for?'

'I don't know.' Lester bit his lip. 'This isn't my speciality, you realize. I've just had a bit of knowledge rub off on me. If I had to make a guess . . .'

'Yes?' Murray prompted.

'I'd say it might be some kind of field-sensitive antenna. See here.' Lester made compasses of his thumb and forefinger and measured off sections of the embroidery. 'There's definitely a harmonic ratio involved in the design, isn't there? The longest straight runs might be a dipole – like a TV aerial.' He shook his head. 'Which doesn't explain why it's *here*.'

'Like a TV – Lester, is there any connexion?' Murray pointed at the open back of the television.

'No idea. The tangle inside that set would take me hours to work out. And frankly, with the HT-load it's carrying, I don't fancy poking about in there.'

'Have you *no* idea what's been added?'

'None at all. I said so.' Lester wiped his forehead. 'Tell you one more thing, though – there isn't room for Gerry's stuff. I'd better just put the back panel on again and leave it.'

'Are you going to ask Delgado about it?'

'Well, I'll certainly ask him about this hypnopaedia jazz. You want my honest opinion, though?'

'I want anything I can get. This thing worries me.'

'All right.' Lester stuffed his handkerchief back in his pocket. 'I think it'll turn out that Delgado has a streak of cockeyed mysticism, which he's a bit ashamed of. Nowadays, a lot of gullible people who don't know a diode from a horse's ear fall for slick operators who claim revolutionary breakthroughs in – ah, what's the word? – bio-electronics, that's it. A few high-sounding phrases about tuning in on the cosmic wavelengths, and they hang their tongues out and buy a little black box for a hundred pounds and slick operator bows out, chuckling. My guess is that you're right and Delgado only uses his halfway convincing excuse about sleep learning to cover for a bit of pure nonsense. Like Marie Stopes insisting on turning her bed to magnetic north, you know?'

'You mean that?' Murray hesitated. It was plausible, granted. He'd worked once for a few weeks with someone who exactly fitted Lester's description, who was paying out fat fees to a charlatan for collections of minerals to improve the colour of his aura but hated to admit the fact.

'I'd be inclined to bet on it.' Lester waved towards the embroidery. 'At first glance, you see, that pattern makes a sort of sense. Make it up in copper tube, you might even be able to get TV signals with it. But on close inspection it doesn't figure. It's got just about the right half-baked quality to fit my theory.'

'And the stuff in the TV set, too?'

'More than likely.' As though reminded, Lester moved towards the set and began cautiously to replace the rear panel. 'I don't see how it can be important enough to worry about. Far as I'm concerned, Delgado can believe in table-turning if he chooses. I was telling you when I came in, wasn't I, that what he's doing strikes me as pretty well miraculous?'

'Yes, but –'

Lester finished replacing the back of the television, stood up, and clapped Murray on the shoulder.

'Come off it!' he said. 'I'd have thought you were glad enough to be in on the deal after the bad times you've been through, without bothering yourself about Delgado's cranky notions. Not meaning to be rude, you know.'

Murray forced a smile. 'I ought to have more sense, I guess. You're quite right. Better this than the breadline.'

When Lester had gone out, Murray lit a cigarette and stared at the design on the mattress.

Sure. Very plausible. But somehow I don't feel there's an off-the-top-of-the-head explanation. I think it goes deeper.

He came to an abrupt decision. It was on the level of poking a stick into a hornets' nest to see what would happen, but he was growing impatient; these irksome problems were destroying his ability to sink himself, as the others were doing, in the creation of the play. And he wanted to do that.

He grasped the head of the mattress and hauled on it. The metal thread twanged and snapped as it had done last night. Once more he pulled the whole of the thread free, rolled it up, and tossed it in an ashtray.

Then he went to the cable of the TV set and looked it over. It occurred to him that if it was carrying the load Lester suspected, he had better not hold it directly for what he had in mind. Instead, he picked up the entire set with a grunt – it was much heavier than it appeared – and carried it across the room.

When the cable was taut, he took a fresh grip, and lunged forward, expecting the cable either to break or to pull loose. It did neither. Another six or seven feet of cable emerged from the hole in the floor, and beyond the wall – in room number thirteen – there was a monumental crash. It sounded as though someone had thrown a crate of milk bottles into a pile of scrap iron and brought the lot tumbling.

Murray raised an eyebrow. A smile quirked the corner of his mouth. With exaggerated care he restored the television to its stand and turned back the carpet over the extra length of cable.

Then he went to the door of the room and opened it a quarter-inch. He waited, his eye at the narrow slit. Shortly, he was rewarded by seeing the normally imperturbable Valentine come down the corridor at a dead run.

Well, what do you know?

The door of room thirteen opened and closed. Murray shut his own door and went to put his ear to the dividing wall. All he heard, though, was a tinkling and clanging as though Valentine were picking up the pieces.

Good enough. Now to find out what Delgado's reaction was. He left the room and went whistling downstairs.

10

The reaction came, but though it might have originated with Delgado, it came from Blizzard, and Murray had to wait patiently for it until more than an hour after the end of dinner.

There was rain rattling at the windows. Keeping up a desultory conversation with Adrian Gardner, he listened to it and was struck by a casual thought. Everyone was here apart from Blizzard and Delgado; the group was becoming almost agoraphobic. No one had suggested going to explore the local pubs, or even walking around the grounds during the lunch break, either yesterday or today. The shower, and the breeze which had brought it, might have been an Arctic snowstorm.

Go for a drive after dinner tomorrow night, maybe. Don't want to box in my mind completely . . .

'Murray, I'd like a word with you. Excuse us, Ade – it's important.'

With a start Murray returned from his private musings. Blizzard had appeared and taken a chair facing him, and Adrian, shrugging, was getting up to go and talk to someone else.

'Yes, Sam – what can I do for you?' Murray said.

'You can stop being a damned nuisance, if you really want to know,' Blizzard answered. He took a cigar from his pocket, bit off the end, and spat the fragment into a handy ashtray. There was a table lighter within reach; he picked it up and lit the cigar.

Murray waited till he had finished. Then he said, 'Sam, if you're trying to get my back up, I warn you, you won't like it when you succeed. How am I supposed to be a damned nuisance?'

'Have you been mucking about with the TV set in your room?'

'I thought I might prefer it on the other side of the bed,' Murray said blandly. 'If that's "mucking about", I'll confess to it cheerfully.'

Blizzard looked at him intently. But his professional mask was proof against the scrutiny. Finally the director gave a sigh.

'Well, for Christ's sake don't do it again,' he said. 'I had Valentine come to me practically in hysterics. Look, all the sets upstairs are connected to a rediffusion system. Apparently you hauled on the flex of your set, and it pulled over a stand of equipment and smashed about fifty quid's worth of valves and junk.' He wiped his forehead. 'Murray, I don't have to tell you that there's more money behind this venture than anything else I've ever tangled with. But it's not a bottomless supply, you know.'

'So it's supposed to be a rediffusion system,' Murray nodded, ignoring the last part of what Blizzard had said. 'How odd. Lester didn't think it was.'

He cocked one eyebrow, preserving the most innocent expression he could contrive.

'Lester! So that was your doing, too. Murray, what the hell *are* you playing at? Is your vanity hurt or something? Because if you don't like it here, I'm sure we can –'

'Just a second,' Murray cut in. The near passion in Blizzard's voice had taken him aback. 'What am I alleged to have done to Lester?'

'He came to me before dinner with some kind of solemn warning about Delgado.' Blizzard shot a rapid glance around the room to ensure he was not overheard. 'He was saying he thinks Delgado is a crank of some kind because of these tape-decks in the beds that you were kicking up a stink about last night. Murray, will you please do me a favour and shut your big mouth?'

Murray tensed. He leaned forward. 'Sam, are you trying to run this place like a concentration camp? Are you putting a ban on curiosity? Jesus, you know the kind of people we have here! You want hysteria?'

'No, that's precisely what I don't want, and it's also what you're in a fair way to causing. Listen to me, Murray. We know each other pretty well – we've worked together before – so you won't misunderstand me unless you deliberately want to. I'm no happier than anybody else with this notion of cramming a dozen highly-strung people under one roof and then working them up to fever pitch. I've never heard of anything like it before. But it happens to be Delgado's preferred method of tackling things, and if he wants it, I want it. What's your impression of Delgado so far, Murray?'

'I'm still working it out.'

'I've been involved with him – and his backers – for about four or five months.' Blizzard tipped the ash off his cigar. 'I know what I think about him. The man is a simon-pure, twenty-four-carat genius. He makes my skin crawl, but he also makes me shiver with awe. Ever hear me say that about anyone else, Murray?'

'No.'

'So you see what I mean. He has fantastic talent. He has incredible money behind him, from some Argentine billionaire who apparently wants to prove some point about his country's culture by selling it to Europe. I have to keep this gang of neurotics under control – ah, sorry! It slipped out, Murray.'

'We're all neurotic,' Murray said without humour.

'Yes. Let me get on, anyway. The point I'm making is that I don't want irrelevancies to foul us up. If Delgado wants to use this sleep-learning gag, let him, because neither you nor Lester nor a gang of professors will make me interfere. And does it *matter*, anyway? If it works it works, if it doesn't why should you worry? I'm not banning curiosity, as you put it. I'm trying to keep the project on the rails.'

Murray hesitated. There was such naked emotion in Blizzard's voice that he felt slightly ashamed of himself. It hadn't been necessary to pull the cable of the TV and smash fifty pounds' worth of gear, after all; there was no good reason to take Lester's word about a rediffusion system instead of Blizzard's – Lester wasn't a TV repairman, only a lighting engineer with a hobbyist's interest in electronics.

He said at length, 'You could have started off better, Sam. I haven't any illusions left about myself. Don't think I'm ungrateful. I'm glad to be involved with this. But on the strength of the film Delgado made, and his work in Paris, you could have asked for Fleet Dickinson, or . . . Or could you?'

He hadn't meant to finish in those words. But a memory of what Roger Grady had told him crossed his mind: something about getting a flat no from someone to whom he wasn't even making an offer.

Fortunately Blizzard was prepared to take his suggestion at face value. 'It's not quite like that, Murray. Delgado is authoritarian as hell – you've noticed? He does it cleverly, and he's so transparently right that so long as you're caught up in his enthusiasm you don't mind. But I've worked with Fleet more times than I can remember, on things like *Absalom's Father* and our modern-dress *Lear*. He's used to being boss.'

He broke off. 'Odd! You know, it just hit me, Murray: this is the first time I've seriously talked about what we're doing with you, or Ida, or Ade – in fact, with anybody except Delgado. I don't know what the hell's come over me.'

'He's come over you,' Murray said. 'I'm a bit worried, Sam. I mean, it's good to know you have such confidence in the guy – we're going to need confidence if we're to turn out a West End production from where we are now. For Christ's sake don't lose your objectivity. I can see us going up with a stinker, and we'll all be drunk on it and think it's a masterpiece.'

'I'm doing my best.' Blizzard sounded almost contrite. 'But until I have my hands on this – this co-operatively evolved script, I'm more of a housefather than a director, aren't I?'

Murray frowned. 'Yes.... You know, in spite of the line Roger Grady fed me, about collective improvisation and so on, I didn't really believe it. I expected to be given a plot, at any rate. And then maybe to build dialogue around, the way they do in the Method schools, you know. I was thinking, okay, it's experimental, but it might be an oddball success like that movie – uh – Cassavetes's thing. *Shadows*, that's the one. I surely was *not* expecting to find we had nothing at all.'

'But we have something now!' Blizzard made the words a challenge. 'You can't deny that. And it's after only two working days.'

'Oh, granted, granted!' Murray gave the director a puzzled frown.

'I was concerned about it, too,' Blizzard admitted after a pause. 'Still, it's the way he works, and it seems to be going pretty well. That was another reason for not trying to get Fleet or someone like him, by the way. Fleet is very choosy about his parts – he talks about his "image" a lot, you know? Not even Delgado's reputation would make him buy a part sight unseen.'

'Especially in view of the way Delgado's mind works,' Murray nodded.

'How's that?'

'You know – he said it himself. Cancer and gangrene. I thought it was a form of words designed to shock us into taking notice. But it isn't. He means it. And it makes me feel a bit dirty.' Once again, Murray found himself speaking his mind more fully than he had intended.

'Come off it, Murray,' Blizzard said. 'We do have a sick world, and he does have his own point of view, but it's as valid as Genet's, for example. And I can't imagine you making the same comment about Genet.'

'It isn't the same thing.' Murray stared past Blizzard with

his eyes unfocused, hunting words. 'Genet is obsessed with things that are intrinsically unattractive – buggery and petty theft ... Whereas Delgado has this knack of making things which are perfectly respectable stink in your nostrils. *You* know what I mean. Like lifting up the base of the Venus di Milo to show slugs and wood lice underneath.'

He checked for a moment, and then went on in a lower tone. 'Sam, I don't quite know how to ask you this, but it's been itching my mind, and I've got to. You keep talking about Delgado's personal way of working – well, is part of the idea to coop us up together like a real-life *Huis Clos* until we're all ready to scream, and then put the screaming on the stage?'

Blizzard didn't answer at once. When he did speak, he sidestepped the question.

'What gives you that idea, Murray?'

'Two things. One is what Delgado himself said, about wanting an identification deeper than Method stuff. And the other is the crowd you've picked. Me and liquor. Gerry and horse. Ade and his pretty little boys. Constant grabbing his first chance out of rep and into the West End – his first and probably last, too. A gang of people who can't afford to lose their tempers and walk out, because this is the make-or-break offer, and they won't get another like it in a lifetime.'

'Any time you want to, you can get in your car and go up to town or whatever you like,' Blizzard said stiffly. 'If that's cooping you up, I'm a Dutchman.'

Murray grunted and got to his feet. 'I think I shall do exactly that,' he said. 'The rain's stopped. Some fresh air won't do me any harm before I turn in.'

He was out in the hallway before he realized Blizzard had not given him a straight answer. He was debating with himself whether to go back for one, when Valentine materialized from the dining room.

'Are you going out, Mr Douglas?' he inquired with absolute courtesy.

'Why do you want to know?' Murray countered.

'I have been requested by Mr Blizzard to close the main gate at eleven o'clock, sir. But if you wish, I can arrange for it to remain open for your car.'

'No. No, that won't be necessary. I've changed my mind. I'm not going out.'

'Very good, sir.' Valentine gave a hint of a bow and made to continue across the hall.

'Valentine!' Murray said when he had gone a few steps.

'Yes, Mr Douglas?'

'Do me a favour, will you? Stop fooling around. Stop saying "Mister Blizzard told me." I know as well as you do that Delgado gives the orders, not Sam Blizzard.'

'I – I don't know what you mean, sir.' Valentine's voice was plausibly coloured with surprise, but he betrayed himself by shifting his weight from one foot to the other.

'Then you'd better find out, hadn't you?' Murray suggested, and walked towards the stairs. When, from the landing at the top, he looked around, Valentine had disappeared.

Musing, he made for his room.

Crazy damned setup.... Delgado's a weirdie, and poor Sam's in a flat spin, and I think he half-suspects Delgado's idea is the one I put to him.... But he's right: I'm apt to make it worse if I go on about the tape recorders and the junk in room thirteen.... Okay, I'll pipe down.

But even having reached that decision, he went through what threatened to become a nightly ritual, and stripped twenty yards of fine wire from his mattress before he got into bed.

11

'Okay, everybody. Break now. See you back at – uh – ten to two.'

'Break, he says,' Ida stage-whispered with *Maria Marten* force. 'Me, I'm broken already. Foof!'

Murray drew a deep breath and let it go slowly, feeling the tension ooze out of him. He made a sort of mental check on a calendar in his head. *Thursday: the first time Sam Blizzard gives the order to break instead of Delgado. Maybe we're really going to have a play.*

There was even a title now. Nobody had picked it – just suddenly it had been used. *Upstream.* Not bad. He tried his tongue on it.

We have a set of characters. It's moving. We have Gerry out the back somewhere making canvas flats with his ideas on them . . .

His subvocal recital of the items on the credit side of the ledger stopped abruptly. His eyes had wandered to the back of the auditorium and spotted a figure in shadow alongside the projection booth.

Heather. Good God – she isn't in here yet. She hasn't even been up to the stage this morning.

He jumped down from the stage and went up the aisle to the exit in the wake of Rett Latham, who was putting a debatable point to Adrian with all the emphasis he could muster. He and Adrian both passed Heather with only a nod. Murray stopped, facing her.

'Hello,' he said. 'Where've you been?'

She forced a smile and raised her right arm to show a smear of blue paint on the sleeve of her grey sweater. 'Oh, I went to give Gerry a hand.'

Half the story, Murray decided. The rest of it was in the redness of her eyes. Been having a quiet private mourn. No, this definitely was not fair. Now he cast his mind back, it struck him that no one had made any attempt to draw Heather into either discussions or the extemporization sessions – not even Ida, who might have done it to impress – and her rather appealing shyness would understandably have turned to misery.

'Why?' he said finally.

'Well – you know!' She gave a thin laugh. 'I seem to be sort of surplus to requirement at the moment.'

'What surplus? You were hired, weren't you? So it's your business to remind us that you're here, not dodge off to help Gerry. If he wants help, let him ask for it.'

'I'm terribly sorry. I didn't –' Her mouth compressed, and she looked alarmed.

‘Oh, grief,’ Murray muttered. ‘I’m not trying to snap at you. Just advising you to push a bit harder. Come on, let’s go and have lunch.’

‘No – uh – no, I don’t feel very hungry. I think I’m going out for a breath of air instead.’

‘You know, that’s not a bad idea,’ Murray said. ‘In fact, it’s a damned good idea. How about killing two birds? We’ve got’ – he checked his watch – ‘three-quarters of an hour at least. Let’s go and have a sandwich in a pub. The atmosphere here is getting a bit claustrophobic.’

The girl brightened a little. ‘Oh, I’d love to! If you’re sure I’m not being a nuisance?’

Murray laughed and took her arm. They had just reached the exit when Ida caught them up.

‘Well, well!’ she exclaimed. ‘Is this a private party, or can anyone come? Going to lunch, Heather honey?’

‘Ah ...’ Self-consciously, the girl freed her arm. ‘Murray suggested going out to a pub for a sandwich, actually.’

‘In his *two-seater* car, no doubt.’ Ida tossed her dark-red hair. ‘Watch yourself with him, sweetie. Don’t you know what happens to Murray’s women?’

There was a brief electric silence. Murray turned to face Ida, his hands folding into fists like rocks, his belly suddenly taut as a drumhead.

‘I’d beat the hell out of you if you were a man, Ida,’ he said at last. ‘But you don’t carry things quite that far, do you?’

Again, silence. It was clear to Ida that she’d overstepped the mark, and she was afraid to reply in case she added a last straw. She compromised by pushing between Murray and Heather and going out.

He said nothing further till he excused himself in the hall to fetch his wallet and key ring from his room. When he came back, Heather was waiting with a thoughtful look on her face.

‘Murray, can I ask you something?’

He knew what it was going to be, but he nodded permission as he opened the front door.

‘What did Ida mean?’

‘Ida is a bitch,’ he snapped. ‘You don’t have to pay attention to everything she says.’

'But –' She bit her lip. 'Murray, I don't want to be nosey. But what she said hurt. You couldn't hide it. I didn't want to say anything by mistake which might upset you. So if I do, it won't be deliberate. Uh– I sound silly, don't I?'

He paused, opening the door of the car for her to get in. She met his eyes for a moment before complying. She was a little flushed, as though surprised at what she had said.

He went around the car and got in himself. After inserting the ignition key, he sat for a few seconds in silence. Then, staring at the dashboard, he shrugged.

'What's the good of kidding myself? It's no secret. It's been gossiped about for ages. *Everyone* knows.' He drew a deep breath. 'My wife went out of her mind. She walked off one night when I was at the theatre. They found her two weeks later in a house in Poplar with a couple of tarts and one of London's most prosperous pimps. The only blessing was that she'd given an invented name. She's in a bin, and she'll never come out. Are you satisfied?'

'Oh, my God.' There was no voice behind the words – just the sound of breath. 'Murray, I didn't know! Was that why you –?'

'Why I drank?' Murray turned the ignition key and the engine started. 'No. Not really. I started drinking to quiet my conscience. If I hadn't treated her like a wilful child when what she needed was psychiatric help, she might be well by now. Murray Douglas is a first-class bastard. Better bear that in mind.'

He slammed the car into reverse, spun the wheels on the gravel so that stones rattled under the body like hail, and accelerated down the drive as though fleeing the echo of his own words. At the gate, where he pulled up to let a farm-tractor lumber by, he spoke again.

'And my other bad characteristic is self-pity. Suppose we change the subject, okay?'

Yet by five that afternoon he was prepared to thank her for bringing the matter up. Paradoxically, the old bitterness had coloured his mind during the rest of the day's work – two run-throughs of what was shaping into a complete first act. During the lunch break, Gerry had carried in four flats, the paint still wet on them, and had arranged chairs and tables into a passable sketch for his projected two-level set. He was covered in paint, but grinning like an ape; his exhilaration, in fact, was astonishing to Murray because he had not come to ask for a shot of his drug since Monday night.

He wasn't the only one feeling good. Murray began the first run-through unaware of how his mood was colouring his performance; then he started to catch on, because he was in turn stimulating Ida. During his first few minutes off-stage, he took a grip on himself and planned deliberate exploitation of this hint of bitterness. It felt *right*. It didn't belong to him, Murray Douglas, but to the man he was creating.

He was expecting a possible word of praise from Delgado after the first climax, and he thought the others were too. It had been a tremendous advance on anything earlier. The cast was coming to believe in itself, and the atmosphere was tense. But when Blizzard looking pleased, turned to Delgado and gave him a questioning look, the only comment he received was brusque.

'Again, from the start. Cherry, let me see your notes.'

So they went back to first positions. During the repeat, Murray's mind began to drift away from his body, something that seldom happened to him before a run had reached the point where everything was automatic and the character had taken over his face, voice and gestures. Now, he could already look on with detachment. He could roam away from this first act and consider lines of development for the second and last.

Add, this ... There are fifty similarities and not one hint of identity. Nothing derivative. Hints of Miller, Tennessee Williams – transmuted! Naturalistic opening in a symbolic set with this man, me, Arch Wilde, this curious allusive way his family is a microcosm – of course, it's the two brothers his sons, Al and Rett, which suggests Miller – of a corrupt world when there's not one single word to make corruption explicit, only situations and statements which any audience will recognize and yet the whole, the completed pattern will turn their stomach.... Subtler than Williams; no actual impotence, actual perversion, but this nagging feeling of something being wrong. Like nightmare. Yes, as intangible as nightmare. God, it's frightening.

The inside of Delgado's mind. But he couldn't stop to consider what it must be like. He didn't dare.

Never thought I'd be glad to look so much older than I am, but to have two sons that age, Arch Wilde/me must be forty-five and I haven't had to think myself ahead those dozen years, I've grown into them. . . . It's crying out for overt nightmare now, a Bloomsday treatment with the real characters assuming grotesque proportions and we can use Heather somewhere. . . . Hell of a note if just because she doesn't push herself her first big chance goes phffft. . . . Now I'm over-compensating. But it's true. A few passes from Ida is no substitute for –

'Stop!'

What? Incredulous, everyone looked at Delgado. Blizzard was the first to find his tongue; he, after all, had not been snatched back from probably the deepest level of character-identification anyone on stage had ever achieved.

'Manuel, why in heaven's name –?'

The sallow author was outwardly composed, but there was a veneer of savagery on his voice when he answered.

'I said stop. That's enough. You are beginning to have some idea of the way I want you to take, so tomorrow we will begin again and make the real play.'

'Now just a moment!' Blizzard got up, fuming. There was a chorus of support; Murray raised a hand to still it, and the others complied. Blizzard was obviously going to say what they all had in mind. 'Manuel, you can't mean to throw away a week's work when we're running as smooth as butter!'

'You think so?' Delgado's lidless-seeming eyes lifted with contempt to Blizzard's purpling face. 'There is nothing in it worth keeping. This Murray Douglas you sold to me with such fine words is betraying the concept – not feeling, but acting. He is a shell, and the effect is a piece of buffoonery, not a play.'

'Well, that's a damned lie for a start!' Astonishingly, it was Ida who spoke out hotly. She strode to the front of the stage and planted her hands on her hips, glowering at Delgado. 'Jesus, I'm not exactly in love with Murray, but he's turning in the best performance I've ever seen from him, and you bloody well know it. What's the idea? Are you poking pins in us to make us squirm?'

'You are touchingly loyal,' Delgado said with a sneer. 'But if you're insensitive to what I'm talking about, then apparently you are not fitted to my needs either. Tomorrow, maybe, when you've recovered from your tantrums, we can get down to some work. Right now – Cherry, your papers, please.'

The girl handed him the thick file in which all the notes and drafts for the script had accumulated; they were still working from memory and a prompt copy, but there hadn't been a single line fluffed this afternoon.

'So!' Delgado said, getting up. 'You see I am serious.'

He took the file, which held by now a good hundred sheets of paper, in both hands. With no discernible effort he tore it in half, put the halves together and tore them. In spite of everything, those watching gasped at this display of unexpected strength.

'All right. Now go away,' Delgado said, letting the scraps fall in a white shower around his feet. He whirled and strode up the aisle to the exit.

After a few seconds' stunned silence, Blizzard hurried after him, shouting, and vanished from sight. Murray looked around.

'Anybody got a cigarette?' he said.

'Think he does mean it?' Adrian said nervously, offering a packet.

'Of course he means it,' Murray snapped. 'And the hell of it is, there's not one of us here who can afford to spit in his face and walk away. Is there? God *damn* the man!'

12

There was a pause. At length Murray became aware of an incomprehensible fact. On the faces turned to him were expressions of incredulity.

'Walk out?' Constant Baines said at last. 'Who said anything

about walking out? Look, Murray, just because he tore you off a strip there's no need to go high-horse on the rest of us.'

Murray experienced a second of discontinuity. He said, 'Now wait a moment! What are you snapping at me for? This idiot Delgado –'

'Stop trying to palm it off on him,' Constant interrupted. 'I heard what he said, I heard what Ida said, and the fact remains, he didn't like what you were doing and because of that we have to start over. Fact?'

Jess Aumen, who had remained at his piano, now slammed his hands down in a jagged chord, jumped up, and began to walk along the aisle to the exit. Lester Harkham emerged from the lighting booth and went after him, his shoulders hunched dejectedly.

'You don't think he might change his mind?' Adrian suggested. 'It did seem to me we were doing pretty well. Maybe he just wants to shake us up.'

'Give me one of those cigarettes, will you, Ade?' Ida muttered. 'I think you're kidding yourself. I think the guy's a nut case, and you have as much chance of persuading him to change his mind as – as making the Thames flow backwards.'

'I don't know what's making you take Murray's side,' Constant said harshly. 'That was a very pretty speech you made, but you were all dazzled by going through the motions, and Delgado was watching from down there.' He waved to indicate the seating.

'I – I thought it was very good.' From halfway to the back of the auditorium, Heather's voice came uncertainly. 'I don't know what Delgado had to complain about.'

'Be quiet, Heather!' Constant rapped. 'You've just been hanging around like a ghost since we got here. You haven't contributed anything – you've been a complete passenger. So keep out of it, will you?'

'Constant's right,' Rett Latham said, moving towards the others from the rear of the stage. 'Delgado will stick by what he said, and what made him say it was that he didn't like Murray's performance, and the result is we've wasted nearly a week's damned hard work. Makes me sick.'

There was so much hostility battering at Murray's mind now that he could think of nothing to say. While he was tongue-tied, Gerry Hoading came on the stage, fumbling in his hip pocket. His movement attracted their entire attention. From the pocket he drew and opened a knife. Then he proceeded, his face dead white, to slash across the painted canvas flats he had installed with such pride a few short hours ago.

That achieved, he jumped off the stage without a word and also strode out.

'Well, there's one of us who takes it seriously,' Al Wilkinson commented. 'Rett, let's get out of here.'

'Good idea.'

One by one, then, they moved, with uneasy glances at Murray. Ida was the last to stir; before she did so, she spoke barely above a whisper.

'I think Delgado *is* a nut case, Murray. But – but hell! I guess you'll have to figure out what it was he didn't like that you were doing, or get him to spell it out, or something.'

Murray shrugged. That wasn't the point. If he'd been acting well enough to provoke such approval from Ida, who had no reason to laud him except a straight professional one, he hadn't been deluding himself. He'd been firing on all eight, and Delgado's outburst had had nothing to do with his performance.

Which leaves personal animosity. But why me? Because I've asked awkward questions?

In the aisle, Ida paused and looked towards Heather. In a hard, ill-controlled voice she said, 'Coming, sweetie? Let's go and settle accounts with Constant for what he said to you. It was bitchy of him.'

'It was true, wasn't it?' Heather answered in a subdued voice.

'Come on,' Ida insisted, as though to a sulky child. At last Heather did move, getting up despondently and falling in at Ida's side. That left Murray alone.

He'd predicted that this place was going to turn into a lunatic asylum. Could anyone have picked a surer means of bringing that about? God, it was going to be hell tonight – the temper, the squabbling, the back-biting. And most of it was bound to come his way. For no sane reason. Almost as if Delgado had decided to vent a grudge.

He left the stage, wondering how he could escape the worst of it. No good just going out for the evening – things would be still worse tomorrow, if Delgado stuck to his word and insisted on going back to their starting point . . .

He had reached the rank of seats where Heather had been, about halfway back, and a bit of white caught his eye as he was passing. A handkerchief forgotten on the seat. Absently, he picked it up, feeling it damp to his hand, as though with tears.

Poor damned kid. Why had Blizzard hired her and then been content to leave her out in the cold? It almost suggested that she was an irrelevance, laid on for Ida to get her teeth into in the same way that a supply of horse had been provided for Gerry –

Faint but distinct, the sound of a door closing came from above his head, and instantly every other thought was gone from his mind.

Gerry had said his room must be just about over the middle row of seating. That was Gerry's door.

'God's name!' Murray said, and left the theatre at a run.

There was no answer when he rapped on the young designer's door a few moments later. He went on to his own room; leaving the door open in his haste, he strode to the corner of the window and felt under the pelmet. The little jar of heroin was still there, and at a glance the level didn't seem to have gone down. That was a relief, anyway. Murray replaced it, and turned away slowly.

Yet he still had a sense of foreboding. He came to a decision and went back into the corridor. He put his ear hard against the panels of Gerry's door, and listened, holding his breath.

A tinkle, metal on metal. Another, probably glass on metal. The sound of a match being struck. The sounds built so vivid a picture that he was frightened.

'Gerry!' he shouted, drawing back. 'Gerry, stop that! Don't do it!'

There was no answer. Murray beat on the door like a drum, shouting again.

'Murray, for Christ's sake!' Suddenly the harsh voice of Constant broke on his mind. He had emerged from the next room, number eleven. 'What are you playing at?'

'Give me a hand to break in this door!' Murray rapped.

'Are you crazy?' Constant said, drawing his eyebrows together.

'God damn it, you idiot! Gerry's got a load of horse in there, and he told me himself that if things went badly he'd overdose himself. You going to stand by while he lies dying?'

Constant's face paled. He answered by crossing the width of the corridor to stand beside Murray.

'All right, use your shoulder,' Murray said curtly. 'Hard as you can. On three – one, two, three!'

They hit the door almost together, and the lock ripped jaggedly from the wood of the jamb. There was a long second in which Gerry was turning around from the table on which he had laid out his tackle – an enamel dish with a syringe in it, a jar of white powder identical to the one he had given Murray for safe keeping, and a tiny spirit lamp. In his hand was a cheap teaspoon with the handle bent at an odd angle; his left shirt-sleeve was rolled back above the elbow and his tie was knotted around his arm to swell the veins.

Then Murray had snatched at the spoon, spilling the few drops of liquid it held, and was forcing the hysterical man back towards the bed.

He shrieked and struck out at random until Constant managed to pinion his arms; then Murray slapped him on the cheeks and the fury dimmed in his eyes.

'So it was going to be your second shot,' Murray said after a brief silence. He pointed at a tiny smear of blood already oozing on Gerry's arm.

'Damn you,' Gerry said thinly. 'Get out. Both of you, get out.'

'Not yet.' Murray turned to the table, picked up the jar of heroin and put its screw cap on. 'Constant, look around the room. Make sure there isn't any more of this stuff.'

Constant eyed the jar in his hand. He said, 'Isn't that enough? Christ, I've never seen so much of it!'

'He gave me another jar this size to hide from him. Where there are two, there may be a dozen. Start looking.'

'Damn you,' Gerry said again. 'Get out of my room.' But he was lying back on the cover of the bed now, apparently exhausted. Sweat was running like water on his white face.

Constant didn't say anything, but turned and began to open and rummage in drawers. Murray went to the other side of the room and checked every place he could think of. He drew a blank, as did Constant.

He cast a glance at Gerry, whose eyes were closed now. The first shot had finally hit him, and he would sleep for an hour or so.

'Okay,' he said. 'I guess he'll be all right. But let's take this gear in case he's shamming.' He picked up the enamel dish with the syringe, and the spoon from the floor, and blew out the spirit lamp.

Constant nodded, and followed him into the corridor. He seemed to be trying to form words; at length he managed to get them out.

'Uh – Murray, I guess I should apologize. I don't honestly see why Delgado was so angry with you. I oughtn't to have jumped down your throat.'

'If I'd not been so taken aback, I'd have jumped down his first,' Murray said. 'But thanks anyway.'

Constant swallowed hard. His eyes riveted on the jar of powder Murray still held. 'I – uh – I guess you saved Gerry's life by stopping him from taking a second shot. That right?'

'I don't know,' Murray said uncomfortably. 'Possibly.' Hefting the jar, he added, 'There's enough to kill a regiment in here. He said he was getting it uncut. And you know Will Rogers killed himself with a shot of uncut horse, when he wasn't used to it.'

'But where did he get the stuff?' Constant demanded. 'I swear he couldn't afford that much! Not that I know much about this game, you realize,' he added hastily. 'But one hears things.'

Murray was on the point of answering. He checked. He had just spotted something over Constant's shoulder, through the half-open door of room eleven. A book, lying on the bedside table.

'May I look?' he said, and without waiting for permission went into the room. He set down the things he held and took up the book. He turned to the title page and read aloud.

'Justine: or the Misfortunes of the Virtuous, by the Marquis de Sade, newly done into English by –' He broke off and stared at Constant before resuming. 'By Algernon Charles Swinburne. With one hundred illustrations by various hands. London, privately printed, 1892.'

Constant flushed and spoke in a self-excusing tone. 'It's not mine – I found it here when I arrived. I didn't know it existed. Some of the drawings look like Beardsley.'

Murray turned a few of the pages. Then he dropped that book and bent to examine a shelf similar to the one in his own room. Its contents were very different. *Juliette* was here as well, and *The 120 Days of Sodom*. *My Secret Life*. A very handsome *Fanny Hill*. And at least a dozen more he had never heard of, with titles like *Flagitiosa* and *Put it Down to Exqueerience*.

'You're – uh –' Constant had to swallow again. 'You're welcome to borrow any of them you care to.'

'No thanks.' Murray straightened. 'I have enough trouble with my own little weakness without acquiring someone else's.'

'Don't be so bloody superior, Murray!' Constant said with a touch of his usual acerbity.

'Sorry.' Murray picked up the syringe and the jar of drug again. 'But you were asking how Gerry got his supply of horse. The same way you got those books. He found the stuff in his room. The same way I found enough liquor to tempt a saint when I arrived. You know something, Constant? If you opened up Delgado's skull, I think you'd find he has a sewer instead of a brain.'

13

Very carefully, Murray balanced the enamel dish and the second jar of heroin behind the curtain pelmet. He still hadn't come up with a better idea. He stood back, letting his hands fall to his sides, and was abruptly aware of great weakness. He discovered an ache in the shoulder with which he had charged the door, and as though the ache were spreading into his very mind the trend of his thoughts grew dark.

What'll happen? Tomorrow, will one of these damned black-garbed stewards simply take another jar and another syringe and leave them for Gerry to find, without a word?

He took out a cigarette and began to pace the floor. That must have happened already. What other explanation was there? Gerry couldn't have afforded to buy one such jar of heroin, let alone two. It was on the house.

He felt sick. There was a calculated nastiness in this affair which he was sure could only have originated with Delgado. 'His method of working' – faugh! What did it really consist in: rubbing the nerves of his actors raw?

For the first time, he began seriously to consider the chance of contacting someone who had worked on *Trois Fois à la Fois*.

And yet ... some of the cast seemed improbably eager to jump when Delgado cracked his whip. Take the way in which Constant had swallowed the author's bloody-mindedness and copied him in blaming Murray for the catastrophe. Granted, he'd apologized. But it had taken the shock of seeing Gerry in danger to make him think of being ashamed. Otherwise he wouldn't have opened his mouth, except to make a few more snide cracks.

Even Adrian, the most experienced member of the cast in Murray's view, hadn't contradicted Delgado's ill-tempered attack. Only Ida had done so – and Heather, but she was irrelevant . . .

He felt his mind slide back to the line it had been following when, down in the theatre, he had heard Gerry's door close and then suspected what was going on. He'd been telling himself it was as though Heather were merely 'on the house' for Ida, like Gerry's drug, Constant's pornography, the liquor he'd been tempted with.

It wasn't so silly, that idea. Except – what was the purpose behind it all?

Oh, damn Delgado for a temperamental bastard! Murray strode to the bed. There was only one thing he'd been able to do so far to kid himself he was hitting back, and that was his regular routine of stripping the metal embroidery off his mattress. He'd done it automatically every night since making his discovery, and just as automatically, when the bed was made during the morning, either it was replaced or a new mattress was found. It had happened again; there was the gleaming tracery of wire under the bolster.

He ripped it off. But this time he didn't stop there. He opened the hinged panel concealing the tape-deck, twisted the spools off the turrets, and went to the window. Holding the spool which had less tape, he tossed the other out discus-fashion. It flew a satisfyingly long distance, unreeling a brown tail like a carnival streamer. Then he threw the other one, and slammed the window.

It made him feel better. But it was still a pretty childish gesture. He stubbed his cigarette and took a grip on himself.

Unless he made sense out of what Delgado was doing before tomorrow, there was going to be hell to pay. The resentment the rest of the cast felt against him – conjured up on the author's say-so, but fierce enough despite that – had only started to smoulder. If tomorrow's work went as badly as one could expect, it would blaze. It might ruin the entire venture. But Murray had an obscure conviction that Delgado wouldn't give a damn.

So what was he after? He considered the remote possibility that he wasn't interested in putting a play together at all; he was a character out of one of Constant's books, getting his kicks by making people squirm, with enough money behind him from this Argentine billionaire not to mind if thousands of pounds were squandered.

No, it was too far-fetched. He had made a film which secured critical acclaim. He had made a *succès fou* out of the play with Garrigue . . .

Memory interrupted, in Roger Grady's voice: 'Because Garrigue killed himself. Because Léa Martinez went into an asylum. Because Claudette Myrin tried to murder her baby daughter.'

Would Roger be saying to someone else, next year or the year after, 'Because Murray Douglas started drinking again. Because Gerry Hoading overdosed himself with horse. Because –'?

No.

He was sweating, and his hands were shaking. He drove his attention back to immediate problems. Suppose, for instance, he found himself in this same spot without having annoyed Delgado. Suppose he didn't know anything about the tape-decks in the beds or the mysterious additions to the TV sets.

It didn't figure. It felt wrong. There wasn't any other sane reason why Delgado should have abandoned a play that was going like wildfire on such a specious excuse, except annoyance with the person he attacked. And the only thing Murray had done which had upset Delgado was to ask about the tape-decks.

He was going to look further into this. He had no notion what he might learn, but he had to do something, and no alternative offered itself.

Where to begin? He lit another cigarette and stared towards the wall beyond the TV set, the wall separating his room from number thirteen. The cable was secured now – he'd tested it – so he couldn't deliberately repeat his smashing of a pile of equipment in there. And the door was always locked. He'd checked that, too.

But there was something at the edge of his mind . . .

Got it. He went to the window, opened it, and craned out as far as he could. Yes, that was about right. If Gerry's room was over the middle of the seating in the theatre and his own room was the end one, over the greenrooms, then room thirteen must be over the stage.

He wondered if he could get to its window, but had to abandon the idea at once. There was nothing to give him purchase on the outside wall; the windowsill was a mere ledge, and he could see clearly that the windows were tight shut. You'd need a ladder to get up there. Or a drain-pipe? No, there wasn't one within reach.

So downstairs.

He walked across the stage, having put on the auditorium lights, and stared at the ceiling rather vaguely. He didn't know what to look for. Between the curtain and the flies the ceiling was in deep shadow, and he had to concentrate hard before he could establish details.

It looked as though there was some kind of grille over the ceiling proper.

Glancing about him, he spotted the chairs and tables out of which Gerry had been improvising his two-level set. He measured distances with his eye. If he took up one more chair and set it on the highest table, he could easily reach the grille below the ceiling.

He proceeded to do that.

Beyond the grille something glinted. Bare wires – or metal rods, perhaps; they were quite thick. He got out his lighter and by its wan flame peered and poked with his finger between the bars of the grille.

Nothing he recognized. It was something akin to the metal embroidery on the mattresses. Curves, straight lines, spirals, threw light back to him. They wove between the grille and the ceiling over the entire area of the stage, as far as he could make out –

'What do you find so interesting, Murray?'

Murray started and almost fell off his high perch, having to seize the grille to steady himself. Below him, on the floor of the auditorium, stood Delgado. The sallow face was dark with rage, but the voice had been level enough.

Murray paused. Then he gathered his wits and replied. 'If

you don't know, Delgado, nobody else around here is likely to!'

Delgado took half a pace back, as though from a physical jolt. He said, 'Come down from there, Murray! There's delicate equipment up there, and you've smashed up quite enough already with your damned inquisitiveness!'

Murray cocked an eyebrow. Having startled Delgado, he felt remarkably self-possessed. 'Okay, I'll make a bargain with you,' he proposed. 'You tell me what this stuff is, and I'll stop prying. But I want the truth this time, not a tissue of lies.'

Delgado's response was to mount the stage and lay one hand on the leg of a table supporting Murray. 'If you don't come down, I'll pull this table over and *bring* you down. Don't think I can't do it.'

Remembering the casual strength with which Delgado had torn hundreds of sheets of paper, Murray recognized the value of the threat. There was no alternative to surrender.

'Okay,' he said resignedly. 'I'll come down.'

Delgado stood back. He put his hands on his hips in a curiously womanish gesture as Murray descended.

'I'm getting very tired of you, Murray,' he said. 'You seem to enjoy being a nuisance too much to appreciate that you're here, living comfortably, receiving excellent pay, with the chance of partaking in something which will make theatrical history –'

'Did you write your speech yourself?' Murray broke in. 'Or is it collectively improvised?'

For the second time in the space of minutes he had the unlooked-for satisfaction of discomforting Delgado. Muscles beneath the sallow skin tautened, and the voice took an edge of shrillness.

'What were you doing when I interrupted you, Murray? Why have you been destroying things that don't belong to you? Why are you trying to make trouble?'

'Because you're a very bad liar, Delgado, and an even worse actor.' It was heartening to be able to assume command of the situation, and Murray seized the chance. 'First lie: your story about sleep-learning wasn't true, so I decided to keep needling you to get at the truth. Second lie: your tantrum this afternoon, your saying that the work we'd done had been ruined by me, was so dishonest that even Ida saw through it. Third lie: all this crap about theatrical history! I don't believe you give a damn about creating a play. I think you're an evil little man with a dirty-minded lust for power, and it means more to you to have people dancing when you pull their strings than to achieve something artistically worth while. You may have convinced Sam Blizzard that you're genuine, and you've certainly got talent enough to build a masterpiece out of your material. But I tell you this straight! You won't get me grovelling to you either with threats or bribes. You can feed Gerry his heroin and Constant his dirty books and maybe they'll think you're doing them a favour and be grateful. You won't get a hold on me like that. And if you put your mumbo-jumbo trickery in my bed and stuff mysterious gadgets into the TV sets and lie about what the things are for, you won't stop me digging for the truth. Not until you level with me. Do I make myself clear?'

Delgado had heard him out with unwavering attention, his self-possession seeping back second by second. Now he gave a short laugh, and the sound made Murray's skin crawl.

'You are a very insecure person, aren't you?' he said. 'You have to talk so loudly to reassure yourself. You are afraid that something is going on which you don't understand. You feel that you have missed a clue somewhere, and the idea scares you. So you break things. You can't afford to run away, but breaking things gives you a sense of comforting power. And you shift blame to me because you can't face your own inadequacy. Though I'd have thought it was obvious even to you – after all, it wasn't my fault you drank yourself into the gutter, was it? Still, you have some trace of spirit left. If you did not, I would not hesitate to tell Blizzard to get rid of you.'

'Your technique is showing,' Murray said with scorn. 'To dodge straight questions, you toss out insults, hoping I'll be distracted by a fit of temper. It won't work. You're doing something for which the play is only an excuse, and just so long as you continue to deny that I'll go on trying to prove it.'

'You're obstinate,' Delgado said. 'But I know what I'm doing, and you don't. I don't have to wonder which of us will yield first. As you wish, then. You will certainly suffer unnecessarily, especially when it becomes clear to all your colleagues that you are being deliberately obstructive. However, I can afford to throw you and anyone else aside.'

He gave a sleepy smile. 'And you can't afford to do anything. I'm your last hope, Murray. On your head be it.'

14

My – my head? Oh God, my head!

From a sink of nightmare Murray struggled back towards consciousness, pain like a gong beating inside his skull. His stomach felt acid-sour, and the taste in his mouth was so filthy that to become aware of it gave him a pang of nausea.

Then facts locked together in his mind and he was awake in horror. His eyes snapped open on the grey daylight filling his room. He lay amid a tumbled mass of bedclothes. The air was heavy with stale cigarette smoke and another odour which at first he refused to recognize.

He rolled his head on the pillow; and could deny it no longer.

The bedside table didn't only bear an ashtray full to overflowing with butts. There was a glass on its side, prevented by an empty cigarette packet from rolling to the floor. There was a bottle of gin three parts empty. That was the smell he had recognized.

His hand touched a patch of moisture on the side of the bed. The contact scented his fingers with juniper. There was a smear of lighter colour down the varnished side of the table near him. Fuzzily, he reasoned: from the spilt glass, down to the floor, some of it splashed on the bed.

And it isn't true. God, let it not be true!

Fighting blind terror, he controlled his limbs into purposeful motion. He sat up and put his legs to the floor. Another wet patch there, on the carpet. Across the room, on the floor under the washbasin, another bottle of gin, full, its cap on.

Murray gave a groan and put his head in his hands.

Last night.... What *happened* to last night? His memory held nothing but grey fog. He forced himself to his feet. Crossing the room, he bent to the cold tap and first rinsed the foulness from his mouth, then scooped handfuls of water over his face and head. His mind settled slowly, as though sediment were drifting down in a muddy pool.

'All right,' he said aloud. 'I don't believe it.'

And silently ended: I *daren't*.

Like a stage set. Give the job to Gerry Hoading. Convey that the occupant of the room is an alcoholic. Everything in plain sight. Something glinting on the floor by the bed, A few slivers of glass from a broken tumbler, most of which was piled in the ashtray, accounting for its over-fullness.

Was this a trick of Delgado's? This cynically bitchy *evil* trick? Because he hadn't spent last evening drinking. He clung to that conviction even though there was no memory of anything else to fill the foggy vacancy in his brain. Nothing could have driven him to the suicide road again – not all Delgado's taunts or the scorn and hostility of the rest of the company. *Nothing*.

Therefore an article of faith: by whomever, for whatever reason, he had been framed. The assertion was like a baulk of timber to a sailor overboard in a storm. As soon as he secured a firm grip on it, he found that he could reason with his normal clarity.

Not sparing the time to examine motives or methods, he concentrated on himself and his surroundings. The first new point to strike him was that the headache felt on waking was gone, so quickly it was hard to recall how fierce it had been. Illusion? Ridiculous, but...

He rubbed his tongue around the inside of his mouth. The foul taste, too, had disappeared without his having to scrub it away. When he had really been drinking, he'd had to load his toothbrush three and four times with the most strongly flavoured paste on the market before ridding his mouth of the overnight sourness.

That relieved him of one horrifying possibility, which up till now he had refused to face seriously: that someone had given him alcohol as Gerry took heroin – intravenously. He could scarcely credit that anybody, even Delgado, would wish him a drunkard again, but the evidence insisted. He scanned his body closely, hunting the trace of an injection, and found no signs.

A dream? The hope rose and fell in the same heartbeat. He could have dreamed the headache, the foul taste, the nausea – all those were frighteningly vivid in his real past – but he hadn't dreamed the spilt gin, the broken glass. With determination he set about investigating the concrete traces.

Something gleaming on the tumbled bed. A thing like a coin – his hand touched it, and it wasn't a coin. The cap of the open gin bottle, dull-shining. He seized it, meaning to hurl it violently away, and misjudged his reach so that he pulled up a handful of the undersheet as well.

Revealed was the familiar, maddening tracery of wire embroidery which he had by routine torn off last night.

And yet . . .

Wait a moment. I tore it off early in the evening, long before I turned in, even before I saw Delgado in the theatre. I threw away the spools of tape, too!

Without rational reason, he wrenched back the mattress and exposed the tape compartment below. There was fresh tape in place; the turrets must have been turning steadily for hours, for all but inches had wound to the right-hand spool. And the gossamer-fine wire linking the tape-deck with the mattress was intact.

For a crazy instant Murray swam in a sea of speculation: this tape, his misty memory, the stage-like setting to which he had awakened. Then he calmed, knowing that he had to have proof to support his trust in himself, and seeing a way in which he might secure it.

He looked at his watch. Not yet seven o'clock. He began to wind the spindle, formulating his plans. A doctor. Some way of telling if there was alcohol in his bloodstream. Breathalyser, urinalysis – he'd seen it done at the sanatorium often enough. Blood sample, even. And if it turned out he was deceiving himself, and there was alcohol in his body, he would come back and find Delgado and the hell with what might happen afterwards, beat him till he crawled. Say what had been done, make the others know what a filthy sadist . . .

He checked his thoughts deliberately. Because if he went on thinking on those lines, he had to answer the alternative question, too: what to do if his belief was confirmed, and he had not been drinking last night.

He seized his clothes and hurried them on, put key ring, money, handkerchief in his pockets. No use trying to clean up the room, but he could pour away the rest of the gin and open the windows to flush out the smell. He did so hastily, and then went into the corridor.

As he pulled his door shut, room thirteen opened and Valentine emerged. He moved so swiftly on seeing Murray that there was no chance of catching a glimpse of the mysterious 'rediffusion equipment' inside.

'Good morning, Mr Douglas,' he said smoothly.

Murray muttered something obscene under his breath and went past.

'Mr Douglas!' Valentine called after him. 'Are you thinking of going out?'

'What the hell does it matter to you?' Murray snapped.

'I would only point out, sir, that the main gate is not open yet.'

Murray stopped in his tracks and swung around. There was no expression on Valentine's pale face, but there had been a hint of smugness in his voice.

'Then open it!' Murray exclaimed.

'I have direct instructions from Mr Blizzard, sir. The gate is to remain closed until eight a.m. And it is not yet seven, I believe.'

'Are you trying to make this place into a prison?'

Valentine looked pained. 'Mr Blizzard was most insistent, sir. I didn't question his reasons.'

'All right, we'll see about this. Which is Blizzard's room?'

'I don't think he would wish to be disturbed, sir. It is still earlier than his usual rising time –'

Murray took a deep breath. 'Blizzard!' he bawled at the top of his voice. 'Blizzard! Where are you?' He went to the nearest room whose occupant's name he did not know and hammered on the door with both fists. The sound echoed along the corridor. 'Blizzard! Come out here!'

'Go to hell,' a voice answered. It wasn't Blizzard, anyway. Rett Latham, by the sound of it. Murray went to the end of the corridor and then out on the landing surrounding the main hall, banging on doors and shouting as he went. From the far end of the landing, one of Valentine's fellow stewards appeared, and started towards him with loud protestations to match Valentine's.

'Keep away from me,' Murray said thinly, 'or I'll pitch you over the balusters, understand? *Blizzard!*'

The door of one of the rooms swung open. Sam Blizzard was there, a robe of dark blue over his pyjamas, rubbing sleepy eyes with the back of one hand.

'Murray! What are you yelling for?'

'Is this a prison?' Murray said vehemently. 'Are these damned black-coated ghouls the warders? That bastard Valentine is trying to tell me he can't unlock the main gate for me!'

'What the hell has that to do with me? It's no reason to go screaming about the place fit to wake the dead!'

'So you didn't give him orders to keep the gate shut until eight o'clock?' Murray clenched his fists. He was shaking all over.

'Good God, of course not. Far as I'm concerned it can stay open around the clock. What do you want to go out for at this time of the morning, anyway?'

Murray ignored the question. He swung to Valentine, his teeth set. 'Well?' he forced out. 'What have you got to say to that?'

Valentine's composure had set solid, like a block of ice. 'I'm very sorry, Mr Blizzard,' he said. 'It didn't occur to me that Mr Douglas would disturb you. From his – uh – wild behaviour, I judged it advisable to try and dissuade him from going out. He drives a rather powerful car, and in his present nervous condition . . .'

The door of another room, beyond Blizzard's towards the front of the house, clicked. Murray turned his head. In the opening stood Delgado, wearing an impeccable wine-red dressing gown and Turkish slippers. His hair was combed, and his face bore no trace of sleepiness.

Valentine broke off what he was saying.

'What is all the row about?' Delgado inquired silkily.

'Oh – morning, Manuel.' Blizzard rubbed his face again. 'I don't get it. Murray wants to go out, and Valentine's been spinning him some fool story about keeping the front gate shut till eight o'clock and says I gave him orders.'

A flicker of – dismay? Concern? Some emotion showed on the sallow visage. But the voice was casual.

'Valentine must have made a mistake, then. I suggested shutting the gates overnight. We have a good deal of stuff here that might attract thieves – the bar stock, for example, which is enough to supply a small pub.'

'I'm sorry, Mr Delgado.' Valentine inclined his head. 'I confess I had forgotten it was you and not Mr Blizzard who instructed me.'

'All right, since you gave the orders, you tell him to let me go out!' Murray rapped.

Delgado's lidless-seeming eyes studied him. 'You seem upset, Murray,' he said in a voice which was almost a purr. 'What takes you out at this hour, anyway?'

'I'm going – Sam, listen to me, because it's going to be important later – I'm going to see a doctor. *You* know why, Delgado.'

'I'm sure I don't,' Delgado murmured, but his expression was again clouded by a trace of discomfort.

'Damn it, Murray!' Blizzard took half a step forward. 'If you're ill, why didn't you say so? We have a doctor we've made arrangements with – I can get him here in half an hour.'

'Somebody Delgado suggested?' Murray countered, curling his lip. 'No, thank you. I propose to go and wake up the first doctor I can find for myself. And it's not because I'm ill. You ask Delgado why. Now does this creature of his open the gate for me, or not?'

'Sam, I don't think Murray is in a state to –' Delgado began, lowering his voice.

'All right.' Murray spun on his heel. 'I'll smash the gate if I have to.'

'Valentine!' Blizzard barked. 'Go and open the gate. And don't let's have any more of this nonsense. If Murray or anyone else wants to go out you're to let him, understand? And I mean that, Manuel. You're making it difficult enough for me as it is. I entirely sympathize with Murray after the way he was treated yesterday. Get a move on, Valentine! Don't be any longer than you can help, Murray. Today's work is going to be hell in any case.'

He gave a glare at Delgado and went back to his room.

Delgado raised an eyebrow. Murray tensed, wondering if he was going to try some fresh excuse to stop him leaving, but after a moment he shrugged and likewise re-entered his room.

Murray turned to Valentine, feeling as though he had won a long and bitter struggle. But the black-clad steward was already descending the stairs, and there was no clue to his emotions in the solemn rhythm of his gait.

15

Heart pounding, mouth dry, as though making his escape from a deadly enemy, he turned right at random from the main gate, leaving Valentine standing like an inscrutable statue. He had to drive for miles before he came to any kind of a village, and then he found only a crossroads, with a pub, two shops, and a church grouped around it, and a score or so of private houses with well-kept gardens.

In one of those gardens, behind a neatly clipped privet hedge, a heavily built woman in tweeds was poking weeds out of a flower bed with a walking stick. He jammed on his brakes.

'Excuse me!' he called. 'Is there a doctor near here?'

'A doctor!' the woman said in a county voice. 'Yes! About a quarter of a mile further on you'll see a nameplate on a gatepost. It's on this side.'

He flung a word of thanks and accelerated away.

A thin drizzle began to spot his windscreen. By the time he caught sight of the promised nameplate it had thickened to steady rain. Oblivious, he got out of the car and hurried up the path to the doctor's door.

To the nervous, pale-faced woman who answered his ring, he said, 'I have to see the doctor. It's very urgent.'

The woman put her hand to her mouth. 'Oh dear. Dr Cromarty is having his breakfast. The surgery is open at –'

'I don't care when the surgery is open. I have to see him immediately.'

'Is it – has there been an accident?'

'No. Please! I can't explain. It's just desperately urgent. And I'll pay whatever it costs.'

'Oh dear. Well, I suppose you'd better come in the waiting room, Mr – Mr –?'

'Douglas.'

'Goodness!' The woman's watery blue eyes widened. 'Are you *Murray* Douglas? The actor?'

'As it happens, yes, I am.'

'Good gracious! Come in, come in! The waiting room is on the right there. I'll tell Dr Cromarty at once.'

She hurried through a door leading from the hall. Murray didn't make for the waiting room to which she had directed him; he stood just inside the door, his eyes on the direction in which she had vanished. His mind wrestled with the problem of inventing a plausible reason for what he was going to ask of the doctor.

Before he had completed working it out, a man with greying hair emerged into the hall, wiping a trace of egg yolk from a shaggy grey moustache. He wore a tweed suit complete with waistcoat, and a gold watch-chain spread across his belly.

He absently put the napkin with which he had been wiping his lips into a pocket like an oversize handkerchief, and in a quick practised movement drew out, opened, and slipped on a pair of horn-rimmed glasses.

'Mr Douglas!' he said. 'Ah yes – I recognize you from your pictures. For a moment I thought my housekeeper had slipped a gear somewhere. Well, well! Angels unawares, and all that. Here, come into my consulting room and tell me what it is I can do for you.'

Murray complied. Cromarty waved for him to go first into the room, and closed the door. 'What is it, then?' he said, moving towards his chair and indicating that Murray should sit down.

'Dr Cromarty, can you carry out a test to establish the presence of alcohol in my bloodstream?' Murray dropped into his chair, a tight feeling in his guts.

'As it happens, you've come to the right shop – though it's rather an unusual request so early in the day.' Cromarty let his glasses slip down his nose, eyed Murray over them, and pushed them back in place. 'I do that sort of thing for the local bobbies – drunk-driving cases, usually.' His expression changed. 'You haven't been involved in an accident or something, have you, Mr Douglas? Because if so I'm afraid –'

'No, nothing like that, believe me.' Murray passed his handkerchief over his forehead to clear away prickly sweat. 'It's rather hard to explain, but what it comes to is this. I'm rehearsing with the company of a new play at Fieldfare House, the old country club –'

'Oh, yes! I know the place. Shame it closed. Very luxurious, all mod-con. I'm sorry! Go on.' Cromarty leaned back in his swivel chair.

Murray licked his lips. Half a lie would be better than a whole one here. He said awkwardly, 'It's a job that means a lot to me, because I've been out of work for some time – I've been under treatment for alcoholism.'

Cromarty raised his grey-salted eyebrows.

'And of course if my director thinks I'm going back to the bottle he's bound to fire me, and I don't blame him. But the point is that there's someone there who's – oh, I don't know how to put it – jealous, I suppose you'd call him. And he's played a very dirty trick on me. I woke up this morning to find bottles and glasses all over my room. So before the director gets wind of this I've got to prove that I haven't been drinking.'

Cromarty sat silent for a long moment. At last he said, 'And have you?'

'God, no!' Murray was startled at his own passion. 'Nothing on earth would drive me back to the kind of hell I went through!'

'Hmph!' Cromarty shook his head dubiously. 'Well, I'll see what I can do, Mr Douglas. But you realize that the alcohol level in the blood peaks about an hour after the last drink, and after that some people excrete the stuff faster than others. A negative finding at this time of the morning might not prove very much.'

'I haven't emptied my bladder since waking,' Murray said.

Cromarty shook his head again but got to his feet. 'Well, as a fellow Scot, Mr Douglas, I can't refuse you. I just won't promise anything.'

'Negative, Mr Douglas.'

It had seemed like an eternity of waiting. The words were such a shock that Murray snatched the cigarette from his mouth and dropped it on the floor. He scrambled to retrieve it.

'Thank heaven for that,' he said.

'That's within the margin of operational error, you understand.' Cromarty shut the door of the consulting room and sat down at the desk. 'I take it that what you wanted was a note from me to your producer to reassure him, is that it?'

'Yes, that's exactly it.' Murray felt fresh sweat, but this time it was due to relief.

'Very well.' Cromarty uncapped a pen and selected a sheet of headed notepaper from a pile at his side. 'I shall put down the bare truth: that you came to me at' – he checked his watch – 'let's say you arrived half an hour ago, which is near enough, and asked me to examine you for traces of alcohol in the system, and the result of my test was negative. I won't add the qualifications which I'd have to if this were for a law court.'

He wrote rapidly, blotted the sheet, and slipped it in an envelope before handing it over. Murray took out his wallet and put the certificate inside, then made to draw out money.

'How much –?' he began, but Cromarty raised his hand.

'I have great sympathy with people in your plight, Mr Douglas. One of my oldest friends was too fond of his drink, and he made no such recovery as yours. There's no charge.'

With fervent thanks, Murray headed towards the door. Cromarty swung around in his chair and called after him.

'Oh – and one more thing, Mr Douglas. I'd prescribe some good solid food for your breakfast. It's obvious you've been badly shocked by this underhand trick which was played on you. No point in making it worse.'

Murray nodded and went out.

Breakfast was not yet over when he arrived back at Fieldfare House. He could tell, the moment he entered the dining room, that so far it hadn't been the calmest meal taken by the company. At the top of the table Blizzard and Delgado were arguing in low tones; Ida and Heather, sitting a couple of places away, were saying nothing and trying not to look as though they were eavesdropping; Adrian Gardner, Rett Latham and Al Wilkinson were grouped at the other end, their faces morose. When Murray appeared, everyone – even Delgado – turned to look at him.

He had the certificate from Dr Cromarty ready in his hand. With all attention still fixed on him, he strode towards Blizzard and planted the paper in front of him.

'All right,' he said harshly. 'Laugh that off.'

Blizzard read it. During the pause, Murray sent what he intended to be a triumphant glance at Delgado. But the author was leaning back with a sardonic expression, and abruptly Murray's self-satisfaction evaporated.

He realized why, the instant Blizzard tapped the certificate and looked up.

'This is very commendable, Murray,' the producer said shortly. 'But was this why you made that ungodly row this morning – why you kicked up a fuss about getting out the front gate?'

Doom gathered in Murray's mind like a threatening storm. His eyes flicked, first to Delgado, then to Valentine, who stood impassive by the sideboard, coffee as black as his clothes bubbling in a Cona jug next to him.

He had to go on, Murray realized. He was being carried by his own momentum now. It was too late to alter his assumption about Delgado's intentions. Clearly, the visit to Dr Cromarty had caused a hasty switch, but to fall in with this retraction was to admit defeat.

He spoke in a level voice. 'When I woke up this morning I found a bottle of gin by my bed, an overturned glass, and another bottle on the floor. I can't think of any trick more damnable than that to play on somebody in my condition, and I want to know who did it and why.'

Blizzard drew his eyebrows together. 'I see!' he exclaimed. 'Were you afraid it might not be a trick, Murray? Was that why you went to the trouble of getting this?' He tapped the paper before him. 'I agree – it sounds like a bastardly thing to do to you.'

Murray wasn't watching him. He had his eyes fixed on Delgado. He didn't, even so, spot the signal which the author gave to his creature Valentine. Maybe it had been arranged beforehand. At any rate, Valentine moved forward and spoke in a low tone.

'I beg your pardon, Mr Blizzard, but perhaps I might suggest that Mr Douglas had a vivid nightmare. I myself have checked his room, and I found no traces of the kind he described.'

Delgado permitted himself a parody smile, very quickly over, – clearly intended for Murray's eyes only. But as Murray was shaping a challenge, planning to demand of Valentine why he had 'checked' his room, there was an unexpected interruption.

'That's a damned lie for a start!'

All heads turned. Murray hadn't noticed Gerry Hoading come into the room. The young designer betrayed his condition of yesterday only by a slight flush in his cheeks and an unnatural brightness in his eyes. He was impeccably dressed and his skin had a clean, scrubbed look.

'I heard what Murray said, and I heard what Valentine said,' he went on. He planted his hands on the back of a vacant chair and leaned over it as though to emphasize his words. 'And Valentine's lying. I went to Murray's room when I got up. I wanted to say – well, that doesn't matter! I wanted to see him about something, that's all. And I didn't get an answer when I knocked, though I was sure I'd heard movements in the room. So I watched the corridor from behind my own door, and I saw this – this creep of a steward come out with a couple of green glass gin-bottles. I'm *telling* you.'

Murray felt an overwhelming surge of relief. There had been a long dreadful second when he wondered if in fact proof was going to be given him that he had imagined it all.

He glanced at Delgado. The sallow face was contorted with fury. Like the sarcastic smile of a few moments back, the expression was brief. But this time it wasn't deliberate, for his benefit. Murray drew a deep breath.

'Valentine?' Blizzard snapped.

The steward, very pale, said, 'I apologize, sir. I am aware of Mr Douglas's unfortunate condition – he left no room for misunderstanding when he ordered me to remove all liquor from his quarters the day of his arrival. I can only say I was being misguidedly discreet.'

'Sam, I think you and I had better go and have a word about this in private,' Delgado said, colouring his voice with plausible concern now. He pushed back his chair.

'Sit down!' Murray thundered. 'We're going to have this out in public. Sam, you listening to me? I'm accusing Delgado of putting that liquor in my room – either doing it himself or getting Valentine to do it – and then backing down because I insisted on going to a doctor, but still hoping I'd make a fool of myself and give you the impression I was having delusions. And except for Gerry here, isn't that what would have happened?'

He thought for a moment that he was getting through. Then, sickly, he read his failure on Blizzard's face. The director was so mesmerized by Delgado's personality that he had dismissed the accusation out of hand.

'Douglas is overwrought,' Delgado said smoothly. 'I'm not surprised at this wild attack on me. It was obvious yesterday that he was unreasonably angry about my decision to abandon the existing draft of the play. Apparently he regards a fresh start as being too much like hard work.'

'You can insult me till you're blue!' Murray rasped, feeling his nerves grow raw. 'Somebody put that liquor in my room and tried to make me believe I'd been drinking it and suffered a lapse of memory. It didn't get there by itself.'

'No, clearly not. But a much more likely explanation is that you staged this little drama yourself, to impress Sam.'

The barefaced audacity of that one was too much even for Blizzard to swallow. He said, 'No, Manuel, I'm not wearing that. But I don't want to start a witch-hunt among the company. I don't accept Murray's accusation against yourself, but I can't imagine him doing it himself, either.' He stood up. 'Come on. You suggested that we discuss this privately, and I think it would be better that way. Murray, you sit down and have some coffee to calm yourself.'

'But –'

'Do as I say. I appreciate you're upset, and I'm very sorry about what's happened. But right now you aren't making much sense. I'll get to the bottom of this for you, don't you worry.'

16

'I think it's a load of crap,' Rett Latham said dogmatically. 'I think Murray got stinko last night in his room by himself and this morning he had qualms of conscience.'

'Shut up, Rett!' Ida said. 'Hasn't it worked through your ivory skull yet that that's why he went to see this doctor in the village? The doctor said he hadn't been drinking, and Sam Blizzard has a certificate to say so.'

'What good is a blood test or whatever he had so many hours afterwards?' Al Wilkinson demanded. 'Some people get over the effects quicker than others, and a lush is probably quicker than anybody.'

'I believe Murray,' Heather said with defiance. 'Delgado is trying to make out that he staged the thing himself – but why should he?'

'This griping's getting on my nerves,' Constant said sourly. 'Why should Delgado want to do a thing like that to Murray? That's a much better question!'

'If you want the answer I can give it to you,' Murray flared. 'Stop flapping your mouth and start flapping your ears for a change.'

'Oh – brilliant!' Constant grunted, stubbing a cigarette in a handy ashtray. 'Who's doing your script today, Murray?'

'Constant, for Christ's sake,' Ida said. 'If Murray's got an explanation, listen to it.'

'Okay, I'm listening.' Constant folded his arms with elaborate pantomime.

'To start with.' Murray took a deep breath. 'You don't honestly think Delgado's abandoning the play was due to my acting. You told me so last night, remember?' A protest died stillborn on Constant's lips, and a reluctant nod took its place. 'He has a personal gripe against me. The only thing I've done which nobody else has is to stumble across some peculiar gadgetry in the bedrooms which Delgado can't or won't explain. I've been ripping off the nonsensical bits of wire he has on the mattresses, for example. I –'

He broke off, thinking from her expression that Heather was going to say something, but before she could respond to his look of inquiry Adrian Gardner had jumped into the pause.

'Not your damned tape-decks again! Murray, you're getting to be a bore about them.'

'Agreed,' Jess Aumen said from his stool at the piano. He had been occupying himself with his habitual silent 'practice', and Murray hadn't thought he was listening.

'It isn't just the tapes,' Murray said. 'There's stuff in the TV sets, and there's something in room thirteen. And there's something *under* room thirteen, too. Lester, did you know that there's a sort of giant version of the stuff on the mattresses up there over the stage? It's behind a grille on the ceiling, but you can see it from close to. Go and take a look.'

The lighting engineer shook his head, leaning back in one of the padded seats. 'You know my opinion of this stuff, Murray. I think it's a lot of pseudo-scientific rubbish and nothing to make such a fuss about.'

'Delgado doesn't think so,' Murray snapped. 'It was when I was poking at it yesterday that he –'

'Told you not to, and got you so worked up you decided to get your own back?' That was Rett Latham again, registering boredom. 'Murray, this is all doubletalk. You haven't made the case you said you were going to, and frankly I'm tired of the argument.'

'Hear hear!' agreed Adrian, and ostentatiously checked his watch. 'I wish Sam and Delgado would stop wasting time on this red herring of Murray's and come and join us.'

'I think that's disgusting, Ade,' Gerry Hoading exclaimed. 'It was the most sadistic bloody trick imaginable, what was done to Murray, and you call it a red herring – God, do you imagine he enjoyed it?'

'We don't have to ask why you're taking his part, do we?' Adrian said, curling his lip.

'What's Delgado bought you with, Ade?' Gerry whispered, tensing as though to rise and hurl himself bodily forward. 'An endless supply of pretty little boys?'

'Oh, for Christ's sake can it, will you?' Jess Aumen shouted, swinging around on the piano stool. 'You'll drive the whole bloody lot of us up the wall if you go on!'

Murray recognized the truth of the warning. He yielded despondently and walked to the side of the auditorium, where he put his forearm on the wall and leaned his head against it.

The air smelt sour with tension. Obedient to Dr Cromarty's instructions, he had contrived to force down some breakfast when Delgado and Blizzard had left the dining room, but now he was thinking it had been a mistake; it lay heavy as lead in his guts.

Jesus, how did I get into this madhouse?

He grew aware of someone standing beside him, and raised his head. It was Gerry, a cigarette thrust between his pale lips. Fumbling for a light, the designer said, 'Murray, how the hell did you stop yourself from beating Ade's head in?'

'I don't know,' Murray said shortly. Out of all those here, he would perhaps have picked Gerry last as his staunch advocate, but as a result of last night the matter was settled. 'I don't know. Maybe because the only reason I can think of for Delgado to do as he's doing is to provoke that kind of row.'

'Yes.' Gerry got the light to his cigarette at last. 'Yes – but what *for*? Just to add a real-life tang to his play? It seems crazy!'

'I think he is crazy,' Murray muttered. 'But then, so are we all, to be putting up with him.'

There was a sudden stir. Everyone swung to look at the far end of the auditorium. Murray's heart turned over, and he clenched his hands at his sides.

Blizzard was coming down the aisle, followed by Delgado and the author didn't look his best. His forehead was distinctly shiny, and he was smoking one of his king-size cigarettes not with his usual aplomb but as though sucking comfort with the smoke.

'Sam put up a better fight than I gave him credit for,' Murray said under his breath to Gerry. 'Look at Delgado!'

Gerry nodded, betraying excitement. 'You don't imagine he's got him to back down, do you?' he murmured.

'That?' Murray gave a bitter chuckle. 'Oh, I doubt it.'

But that was exactly what Blizzard had done.

He didn't have to call for attention when he clambered up on the stage. There was an intense silence, broken only by the sound of Delgado's cat-light footfalls crossing the stage towards a chair at the back.

'All right, I've been having a long discussion with Manuel,' Blizzard said. 'You all know about this thing that happened to Murray this morning – yes? I see you do. I don't know who was responsible, but it was presumably one of you lot here, so I know I'm getting through when I say it was a filthy, disgusting, sadistic trick. In spite of certain opinions to the contrary' – he didn't look at Delgado, but no one could doubt whom he meant – 'I think Murray has done bloody well to climb back out of the mess he got into, and he's worked bloody well since coming here, too. I'm going to put it down to the way we all felt yesterday as a result of – well, of what happened. But if there's any repetition, the person responsible goes out on his ear, and I will undertake to see that his membership of Equity is cancelled immediately. He'll never get work in this country again. Is that clear?'

He glanced around the auditorium, scowling, and finally turned to Murray. 'That satisfy you, Murray?' he asked.

'The person responsible won't be worried by that kind of threat,' Murray said. 'He isn't in Equity.'

'Shut up, Murray!' said Constant from the side of his mouth. Murray shrugged and leaned against the wall.

'Murray, I know what you mean by that,' Blizzard said. 'But I think everyone else here would rather I pretended not to.'

'Hear hear!' – in a subdued voice from Rett Latham.

'All right, let's get on. That isn't the only thing I've been talking to Manuel about. We ran over the problem of the existing draft of the play. Manuel?'

The author stirred on his chair. It was obvious he didn't like what he had to say, but he was having to put up with it. Murray's estimate of Blizzard rose afresh. 'Sam has represented to me that it may be possible to salvage what we have so far,' he said. 'I'm willing to concede that quite a lot of effort has gone into it, and a bad lapse on the part of one of the cast' – his eyes flickered to Murray and moved away – 'needn't necessarily mean that it all has to go to waste. So I've agreed with him that if he can get a better performance this morning we can go ahead from there. But it will have to be not merely good, but *damned* good. Clear?'

A wave of relief went through his audience.

'Why the hell couldn't you have said this yesterday instead of mucking around?' Gerry demanded, not sharing the general mood. He strode towards the stage, waving at the big canvas flats which he had slashed last night. 'All that work wasted because of a petty tantrum – God, it makes me sick!'

'I'm sorry about that, Mr Hoading,' Delgado said after a pause.

Murray started. It wasn't like Delgado to apologize straightforwardly. He preferred to find a self-justification, and if possible to make the person he had offended appear to be in the wrong himself. Which implied . . .

'All right, everybody!' Blizzard shouted. 'Places! Ade, I want you and Murray for a minute before we start to straighten out one or two bits I thought were scrappy yesterday. Murray, hear me?'

Belatedly, Murray responded to his name. But as he walked towards the stage, his mind was elsewhere, completing the train of his thoughts.

Which implies that Delgado isn't pretending to care about the play any more. He's yielding there to conceal his real interest.

In what?

17

'If you stop and think about it,' Murray told the air, 'you'll see that there are no end of things – about this place and about us – which are peculiar. Only ...'

He let his voice trail away, uncomfortably aware that he was alone in his room and that if he was going to start talking to himself he would make the situation even worse than it was. He drew on his cigarette and let the smoke out in a ragged cloud that drifted towards the blank back of the TV set.

Maybe it was irrational, but he'd turned the set to the wall. Remembering what Lester had said about it being live all the time, he couldn't escape the sensation of being watched by its blank eye of a screen.

Am I going crazy? Am I crazy already?

He forced himself to tackle the question, not for the first time, and came to the same answer as before: there was someone involved who wasn't sane, and the only other candidate for the title was Delgado. The very idea of the man made his flesh creep now – and yet he hadn't been driven to the point at which he had the guts to walk out. There were too many concrete reasons for staying which outweighed the indefinable terrors he had to wrestle with.

He compelled himself to order his thoughts, and went back all the way to the beginning of the affair.

At first, there had been the suspicion that the venture was absurd: collecting the company under one roof to sweat out the play. Against that, Delgado had a reputation as a successful, even though unorthodox, playwright; Sam Blizzard thought it could be made to work, and he was closer to Delgado than anyone else in Britain; and Murray Douglas needed any job he could get.

The last item still held good. The one before that – ditto. Until this morning, Murray had been inclined to doubt it, but he realized now he had been over-hasty in assuming that Blizzard was completely dazzled by Delgado. The director must be keeping his head to some extent; he knew perfectly well the difference between a fit of bad temper on the part of the author and a real crisis of artistic principle. Today's work, which had gone like a bomb and carried them into a first-class symbolic nightmare of a second act, was proof enough that Sam Blizzard cared about getting out a worth-while play.

For Murray, though, it was also – not quite proof but – grounds for suspecting that Delgado didn't.

Why was he suffering this absurd inchoate anxiety? No one else was taking Delgado at other than face value. Lester Harkham, for example, was ready to dismiss his electronic peculiarities as quasi-mystical mumbo-jumbo not worth a second thought. Blizzard didn't seem to have an inkling that he was dealing with anything but a conventionally temperamental creative personality. Gerry Hoading was taking Murray's view seriously for the moment, but you could account for that by invoking the violent emotional shock of nearly killing himself and being saved by Murray's intervention. Compare Constant's near-affability of last night with his return today to his habitual sarcastic intolerance.

No, there was no single item of evidence to support Murray's suspicions. There was only a list of cumulative subtleties.

People's behaviour, for instance. Thinking about the TV set had brought one point to mind. Murray hadn't turned on the set in his room once since his arrival – not even to catch a news bulletin. He knew why; the additional circuitry hidden inside frightened him. But that didn't tell him why no one else had mentioned seeing any programme on TV since coming here.

And as to news: no newspapers. No one had troubled to order a paper as far as he could tell. No one read anything at breakfast. Why on earth not?

Phone calls. It was probable that the company had been picked partly because they had no domestic ties – well, fair enough; if it was part of the plan to have everyone thrown together around the clock, you wouldn't want people in a hurry to drive home at quitting time or risk them being delayed in the morning by a crisis in the family.

By itself, it meant nothing that everybody here was either single or separated or divorced. But that didn't exclude all personal ties. So why had no one been called to the phone in Murray's hearing? In his own case: why hadn't Roger Grady, for instance, rung up to inquire how things were going? Granted he had no really close friends at the moment, because he had been deliberately avoiding people since leaving the sanatorium; was this a reason why everybody else should receive no calls?

No letters, either. There was a board in the hall next to the room where Blizzard had his office. Murray couldn't remember seeing anyone check it for mail. He hadn't done so himself specifically – he'd glanced at it in passing, but he wasn't expecting letters, and not until now had the point struck him as significant.

There were at least five cars here: besides his own, there were Sam's Bentley, Ida's flame-red Corvette, Lester's Rover, and a Ford drophead that he thought was Jess Aumen's. The rest either didn't own cars, or had left them at home because they didn't expect to be using them much. Nonetheless, five was plenty – surely! Yet no one had suggested going up to town for a show, or a party, or dinner. Like children in a boarding school, the entire company had developed the habit of reporting regularly for every meal, sitting around in the lounge in the evening and having a few drinks, playing records, behaving in short as though they were retired and settled down for the twilight of their days in a quiet residential hotel.

Murray slapped the arm of his chair and jumped to his feet. No, this whole situation was preposterous! How in God's name could you condition a pernickety, temperamental bunch of theatre folk into a placid routine like that?

Oh, true enough: the service which Valentine and his weird aides provided was conducive to comfort – there were no petty problems to distract the mind, like organizing one's laundry or going out for cigarettes. Everything was attended to in a way which a hotel might envy. The food was of high quality, the rooms were indisputably comfortable ... And it didn't figure.

Murray paced back and forth in the space between his bed and the door. At last he had it! This was the source of his worst – though least-defined – anxiety. It had taken a long time to put a finger on it, precisely because it was so vague. Now he could add to the list indefinitely. Tomorrow was Saturday, and at quitting-time this evening it had not been questioned that they should work through the weekend on the same schedule as hitherto. Another oddity. And he remembered the way he had gone out to explore the grounds on his arrival, and the shed full of sports equipment he had found, and the woods at the back of the house. You'd expect a couple of young men like Rett and Al to be interested in the sports hut. The weather had been cool and often showery, but it hadn't been so bad that one had to huddle indoors. There was a hard tennis court, wasn't there? There was the swimming pool – neglected, with leaves floating in it, but certainly not foul or stagnant yet. It wasn't ideal bathing weather, but it wasn't midwinter.

Nobody going out walking. As far as he could recall, the occasion when he took Heather to that local pub for a sandwich lunch was the last on which any member of the company had got in his car and driven out of the front gate – apart of course from his later panicky visit to Dr Cromarty.

Why?

And, thinking of Heather: she, Cherry Bell, who hardly counted because she spent most of her evenings typing up the day's material for Delgado, and Ida, were the only three women here. Everyone knew about Ida. But that didn't stop Heather being very pretty indeed. He had his own reasons for not making up to her; Ade had his, and Gerry's drug-addiction had left him with an eerie near-sexlessness. That still left Rett, Al, Jess Aumen, Lester Harkham – who, though nearly double Heather's age, was handsome and had something of a reputation as a womaniser. Sam Blizzard himself, come to that, with his three – or was it four? – unsuccessful marriages behind him. Not to mention Constant, who had always been chasing girls in the days when Murray and he worked together in rep.

No shortage of susceptible men. Yet because of their apparent total lack of interest in Heather he had been able to formulate the absurd idea that she was laid on for Ida as Gerry had his heroin, Constant his pornography, and perhaps others of the company things that he didn't know about.

In memory, the vivid picture arose of Gerry spitting at Ade this morning. *An endless supply of pretty little boys?*

His head was spinning. This place was sick, with a kind of all-pervading nastiness copied directly from a Delgado play. It was one thing to see it, quintessential on the boards; it was altogether different to be living it, knowing that there was no automatic escape at curtain time, back to the familiar world of long-standing friendships and outside interests.

He checked his pacing and turned to look at the enigmatic squat black shape of the telephone on the bedside table. It had rung for him only once a day since his arrival: each morning at a little before eight, when Valentine's smooth voice reminded him of the time.

Who was Valentine, anyway? His attempts to convey the impression that Blizzard had hired him specially had failed, as far as Murray was concerned. He had a very close connexion with Delgado, probably going back years. Was that clear to Blizzard, or did the director still think Valentine had been his own discovery? And how had it come about that the steward was engaged anyway? A recommendation by Delgado somehow felt like too obvious an explanation –

Murray clenched his fists, his heart hammering. No good letting this thing run away with him. Any minute now he'd be a raving paranoiac, at this rate. Determined to do something either to allay or actualize his fears, he went to the phone and picked it up.

In a moment, there was an answer: not Valentine, but one of the other stewards.

'Yes, Mr Douglas?'

'Get me a call to London.' Murray pulled open the drawer of the table under the phone in which he had put some of his personal effects. He found his address book and turned up the page which bore Roger Grady's home number.

When he had read it over the phone, the steward said, 'Very good, sir. I'll call you as soon as I get through.'

You do that, Murray adjured him silently and put down the phone.

His last cigarette had burned out, forgotten in an ashtray. He lit another, his hands shaking with his absurd nervousness.

Suppose the call doesn't go through? I write a letter, I guess – no, two letters. I think I have stamps somewhere. And I give one to Valentine to mail and send the other myself and ask Roger to call me and let me know if he gets both ...

What a lunatic predicament! For a moment he was suddenly doubtful of his own stability; he had felt this way when he was first in the sanatorium, and the alcohol-hunger grew unbearable, so that he devised elaborate schemes for smuggling drink in.

But that was over, he reminded himself sternly. Somehow, he'd achieved a balance. Now he was too frightened of what drink could do to him to yield to the occasional desire which tormented him – this very moment, indeed, a wave of despair crested, with a demon in an eggshell riding it. The ache was there, God, yes! But so long as the fear of consequent disaster was dominant, he was safe.

And since Delgado's trick this morning, he knew the fear was stronger than ever.

The phone shrilled. He snatched at it.

'Roger?'

'I'm sorry, Mr Douglas. There is no reply from the number you gave me.'

Liar – ? Murray checked his watch. A quarter to eleven. No, it was entirely possible that Roger was out. He dared not assume persecution without impregnable evidence.

'All right, thank you,' he said in a dull voice and lowered the phone.

What now? Write that letter? It wouldn't arrive till Monday, of course. Better to try another call – say in an hour. Roger wasn't an early bird. He could put up with ...

There was a knock on the door of his room, and his mouth went so dry that he was barely able to choke out a question as he swung to face the blank panels.

'Yes? Who is it?'

18

The door opened. It was Heather, in jeans and a white nylon shirt just translucent enough to let one guess that she was wearing a white bra. She looked incredibly young, the more so because her only make up was a trace of lipstick, and she was rather flushed.

'Murray?' she said uncertainly. 'Am I disturbing you?'

'No, for heaven's sake. Come on in.' He hoped devoutly that the relief he felt didn't show too clearly in his voice.

She closed the door and paused a pace away from it. 'I – uh – I wanted to talk to you,' she said. 'I wanted to ask you some advice. I've got to ask somebody.'

Grandpa, Murray said sourly under his breath. *Thirty-two, and they're coming to me for advice already*.

He covered the momentary bitterness by waving her to the one easy chair and turned aside to stub his cigarette half-smoked.

She took the chair, leaned back, clasped her hands around one raised knee and spoke with forced brightness, as though delaying the utterance of what she had in mind.

'Well, it went better today, didn't it? That must be a load off your mind.'

'And on yours.' Murray flipped open his cigarette case and held it for her to take one, then fumbled for his lighter. As she bent to the flame, she seemed to hear, a few seconds late, what he had just said. She checked the movement.

'What do you mean?' she said, raising bright large eyes as nervous as a fawn's.

'Just that. You wouldn't be human if you hadn't been hoping that starting clear from scratch would give you a chance to dig yourself in instead of sitting at the back of the room or sliding away to help Gerry.'

'You make me sound horribly mercenary,' she said after a pause. 'If that's the way I strike you, I'm sorry.'

'Wasn't that part of what you've got on your mind?' Murray hooked his toe around the leg of an upright chair and sat down facing her.

'Ohhh! Oh, yes in a way I suppose it is.' She wasn't looking at him, but at the back of the TV set, perhaps not liking to ask why it was turned to the wall. 'I just don't know what to do, Murray. I'm strictly a fifth wheel. It wasn't important at first – I thought, well, I'm lucky to have this kind of break anyway even if it's only sort of educational, and if I get left out of the final production, so what? I'll have had a month or so at rates double what I've been getting in rep, and I'll have learned a lot just by being around Delgado and Sam Blizzard and you. But I can't feel so optimistic about it any more. There's something so – *planned* about it.'

Startled, Murray jerked his head. 'What do you mean?'

'I can't put a finger on it.' She made a helpless gesture. 'It's just that Sam doesn't seem to be worried – I mean, he hired me, so presumably he wanted some work out of me, but he hasn't said anything, not even bawled me out for making myself scarce occasionally. And you're the only person at all who's made any comment about it. No one else seems to find it at all odd. Although Ida –'

She broke off. Before Murray could prompt her, she had made a face and looked with distaste at her cigarette.

'I'm smoking too damned much,' she said, stubbing it. 'Oh God, I've made my throat so dry. Can I have a glass of water?'

'Sure.' Murray got up. A thought struck him as he made to go to the washbasin, and he turned to the wardrobe instead. The dozen cans of fruit juice were still on the shelf, untouched since Valentine put them there. He picked up one of them and showed it to Heather.

'Like one of these instead? They're just sitting here doing nothing.'

She nodded, clearly not caring what he gave her, and he punched holes in the can with his pocket-knife.

'You were saying something,' he invited as he poured the juice into a glass and handed it to her.

'Thank you.' She drank thirstily, downing half the juice at one go, and leaned back in the chair again. 'Yes. Well . . . I thought I might ask you because you've been rather nice to me, and you seem to have more – oh, this is ridiculous, but I can't think of any other way to put it! You've got more initiative than the rest have. I mean, everybody but you seems to be so passive, sort of chained to a routine. This isn't what I was expecting. You know? Just work all day, half-hearted gossip all evening, and that's it. I don't feel I've got to know anybody. I don't feel that anybody is excited, or even more than vaguely interested in what we're doing – except you. You've poked around and asked awkward questions and found the tape recorders in the beds and things – am I making sense?' She broke off and looked at him with barely-veiled fear.

'All kinds of sense,' Murray said grimly. 'Go on.'

She emptied her glass and set it down beside her. 'You know something? Ever since you showed me that weird gadget in my bed, I've been worrying and worrying. Nobody else seems to care – they just pretend to be bored if you mention it, don't they? But every night when I go to bed I turn down the sheet and – and I cut the little bit of wire joining the mattress to the tape recorder. With my manicure scissors.' She laughed. 'Isn't it silly? But the idea of that thing unwinding all night under my head – it just bothers me. Is something wrong?'

'No. No, quite the opposite.' Murray was staring at the far wall, his eyes unfocused. There was something vitally important at the edge of his mind, triggered by her words. 'I do the same, only more so. I keep pulling the wire embroidery off my mattress and throwing it away. It's always put back, but it must be a damned nuisance. Which is why I'm doing it, I suppose. I want to make Delgado lose his temper and admit what it's for.'

'You're sure he was lying when he said it was –?' She fumbled for the word.

'Hypnopaedia? Of course I'm sure. Even Lester said so when I showed the stuff to him. But he doesn't take it seriously – says it's some kind of pseudo-scientific magic that Delgado believes in.'

She licked her lips. 'Could I have another glass of that fruit juice? I'm still thirsty.'

'Surely.' He rose to get it for her, and opened a second can and left it near her.

'Is the fact that you've turned your television to the wall something else to do with Delgado?' she asked at length.

'Very clever of you,' Murray said dryly. 'Lester found some more electronic gadgetry in there . . . It's permanently live, and you can't turn it off. I have this ridiculous feeling it's watching me. So –' He grimaced and shrugged.

'Yes. I know what you mean.' Her voice was very serious. 'But what's it for? What's the idea? I can't get anybody to help me wonder!'

'I don't know,' Murray said. 'All I do know is that Delgado is far more concerned about things of that kind than he is about his play or losing money or anything else straightforward. Was that what you wanted to talk about, by the way?'

'No.' She drained her glass again and reached for the second can. On the verge of pouring from it, she glanced at him. 'Oh – am I taking your whole supply?'

'Go ahead. Drink all you want. I haven't touched it yet, and somebody might as well use it up.'

'Thanks. It's very good, actually.' She filled her glass. 'Do you want some?'

He shook his head. 'Go on. It's a relief to find there's someone else worried about the same things as I am.'

'Well – not entirely,' she corrected. The colour came back to her cheeks, brighter than when she entered the room. 'What I'm desperately trying to decide is whether I shouldn't call it off and leave here. Like I told you, I can't kid myself I'm benefiting from a unique and exciting experience – not now. I set such store by this, you know! I've been for auditions and I've pulled all the strings I could – not many, of course, but there were people I got to know at the Gourlay School, and a few people who were in rep with me who'd got to the West End or into films, and I put as much pressure on as I possibly could. And then suddenly this turns up: a Delgado play, the sort of thing people talk about in the same breath as Beckett or Ionesco, and a part specially written – well, that was the interpretation I put on the offer when it was made. Did you notice the stars in my eyes when I got here?'

'I seem to recall I tried to put some of them out,' Murray said in a grey voice.

'It was just as well. I ought to have thanked you for it, actually.' She sipped and went on sipping at her glass of juice. 'If I hadn't had some warning that I was fooling myself, I'd have been much worse let down when I worked it out on my own.'

Murray gave her a curious glance. Her words were quickening and the nervousness was going out of her manner, to be replaced by a puzzling uncharacteristic emotionality. Making a wild guess at the reason for it, he said, 'You wouldn't just want to ask me whether you should stay or not. If that were all, you probably would decide to stay, for your original reasons. To watch a Delgado play come alive from nothing is a chance a lot of people would like, isn't it?'

She gave a harsh laugh. Putting down her glass – empty for the third time now – she retrieved her unfinished cigarette, straightened it, and lit it with her own match. Something seemed to catch her attention as she did this, and she cocked her head as though considering what it had been, but she gave up after only a few moments.

Unexpectedly, she giggled. 'Oh dear!' she said. 'I suppose it isn't at all funny really, and when I came in I was taking it very seriously indeed, but actually it's so *silly*.' She looked alarmed for a second, put her knuckles to her mouth, and failed to repress a loud burp.

'Goodness, what's come over me?' she demanded of the air. 'That stuff must be gassy, I suppose. I didn't think – oh, never mind.'

Got it. Murray sighed and relaxed a little. The explanation for this odd behaviour was so simple he ought to have found it immediately. She'd obviously been trying to lubricate her problem with a few drinks before she came to see him. Now they were catching up on her.

He scowled to himself. Still, he was the last person entitled to read a lecture on temperance – and not everyone was unfortunate enough to slip from social drinker to lush.

He said with patience, 'Heather, it's no good making me guess what you're talking about.'

She looked surprised. 'Haven't I told you yet? I'm sorry. Ida says she's in love with me and wants me to go to bed with her.'

'Weren't you expecting her to?' Murray said blankly. He'd never known Ida to beat about the bush for long; she had a positively masculine impatience with preliminaries. And he'd assumed, too, that Heather was as aware as anyone of the situation. She was young, but she wasn't exactly a convent schoolgirl.

As her next remark underlined. She giggled again. 'Murray, it's impossible to take her seriously, isn't it? I mean, she isn't a bad actress, but when it comes to trying not to act – you know, saying something she really means – she doesn't seem to know how any longer. She sounds as if she's still putting on an act – Oh, God!'

Her voice changed completely between words. She put down her cigarette not quite in the ashtray, but to one side of it, and when it rolled on the table she didn't pay attention; she was staring straight ahead of her.

'Murray, I feel dreadfully giddy. I think I'm going to pass out,' she said with extreme clarity. 'I feel drunk. But how can I possibly be drunk? I haven't had anything all evening except some lager with dinner, and one glass of lager – Oh, *God*.'

She tried to pull herself to her feet, her face drained of all its colour now.

'Murray, you couldn't have.... No, please, you didn't!' She was waving her arms as though trying to get a grip on the air and pull her body out of the chair. 'Ow, I feel so sick.'

Murray moved like a puppet, rising to his feet, helping her out of the chair, making her stumble across the room to the wash-basin, turning the cold water on so that she could suck at the tap and then bend over the white porcelain, her mouth gaping. He left her struggling to vomit and went to pick up the unfinished can of fruit juice on the table. He sniffed at it, spilled a little into the palm of his hand, and with a terrible sense of doom tasted it. The tartness of the juice masked it well, but there was no doubt of what the cans had been spiked with. Just possibly an unflavoured spirit like vodka, but still more likely raw alcohol.

Heather would get over it. But if Murray himself had opened one of those cans, he might as well have been drinking cyanide.

19

For a fearful moment, Murray's mind was crowded with visions of a possible future. If Delgado were so eager to – well, the phrase was true enough – poison him, where would he stop? The tins remaining in the cupboard looked as innocuous as those he had opened for Heather; he scrutinized them and saw no hint of tampering.

What should he do? Take one of the cans and offer it to Blizzard as evidence – of something which Blizzard might refuse to believe? The cans need not all contain alcohol; he might by chance have selected the only two, because they were placed in front of the others and fell under the hand.

And where next? In the glass of limejuice and soda brought to him at dinner by Valentine? Running out of the taps over the washbasin? There was no knowing, and therefore Murray felt himself to be in a kind of Dracula's castle, where from now on every shadow would hold a threat.

And it was shadows he had to contend with, too. There was a grand absurdity in trying to poison an ex-alcoholic with alcohol which he had seen foreshadowed on Blizzard's face when he was presented with Dr Cromarty's certificate. To stay and argue things out offered little hope. He would have to run, and the hell with everything. He felt sick with terror.

Behind him, Heather turned dizzily away from the washbasin; there was a sour smell in the air, and she had left the cold tap running to wash away what she had brought up. He moved to steady her as she went towards the bed.

'Leave me alone,' she said. 'Oh God, leave me alone. I mean it.'

'Heather, I didn't spike what you drank,' Murray said. 'It was meant for me, not you.'

She didn't reply. Possibly she couldn't. If the single taste Murray had taken was any guide, she must have drunk the equivalent of a tumblerful of over-proof spirit in less than ten minutes, and even if she had vomited back half – which he doubted – it would have hit her hard.

She half fell on the bed, one leg trailing to the floor, her head pillowed on her arms. Her breathing was thick and irregular, and after a few moments she started to moan softly.

Murray clenched his hands by his sides. Running was only half the answer. He had been so blinded by his own plight that he had forgotten the obvious: Delgado wouldn't be concerned solely with him, Murray, but with the corruption of everyone in his temporary domain. The plainest example was here before his eyes, wasn't it?

He had to think. He had to plan. Somehow he had to make not only his own escape, but one for Heather at least, and if humanly possible he had to prevent Delgado repeating this –

Click.

Paris. Garrigue's suicide. He had been going to call Roger Grady.

With sweating hands he picked up the phone and told the smooth-voiced steward to try the number again. Then, waiting for the call to go through, he locked the door after a cautious glance both ways along the passage. No one was in sight.

He came back and sat by the phone, his mind once again itching with a point Heather had suggested by implication. She had said she too broke the connexion to the tape-deck under the pillow . . .

He snatched breath in jumping to his feet. As though she were a baby, he lifted her up and turned her bodily around on the bed. She didn't protest. He gently moved aside her feet, so that he could raise the pillows. Yes, the usual had happened. What he had stripped off last night had been duly replaced. It was the merest guess that it might affect the sleeper's head, but it made better sense than any alternative.

Some sort of – electric field? Lester compared the pattern of wires to a field antenna –

The phone went. He seized it, and could barely speak his name for relief when he heard Roger's familiar tones.

'Roger, thank God! Murray here!'

'Oh, you!' The line was not very good, but he could picture the movement that went with the words: a kind of drawing together. 'What the hell do you want at this time of night? You realize that as a result of your poking Burnett in the jaw last week he's mounting a kind of hate-campaign against not just the Delgado play but everything with a spark of intelligence that's –'

'Roger, shut up and let me talk. There isn't likely to be a Delgado play the way things are going.'

'I already have that impression,' Roger grunted. 'I don't know what strings Burnett's been pulling, but they work. You may not get the Margrave after all.'

'The hell with that. Will you *listen*? Roger, this man Delgado is a lunatic. I am not exaggerating. Delgado is a certifiable maniac and ought to be in an asylum. In the past week we've had catastrophes enough to last most productions through a year's run – he's had a fit of pique and torn up the draft and been cooled down by Sam –'

'In that case what are you worrying about?'

'Roger,' Murray said in a tight voice, 'unless you let me finish, I'll climb down this phone and strangle you with the cord. Gerry Hoading has come within inches of killing himself because Delgado's got him unlimited quantities of uncut heroin. The place is full of all kinds of incomprehensible electronic gadgetry which Lester Harkham says is just a load of mystical rubbish – but I'm not sure, because . . .'

His voice trailed away. He'd spotted the point he'd almost had from Heather. Besides himself, she was the only person asking awkward questions about the set-up. She was accustomed to disconnect the tape-deck under her pillow. She, Ida, and Gerry Hoading were the only people apart from Lester to whom he'd directly demonstrated the existence of the gadgets. And, except for Blizzard, those were also the people who seemed least under Delgado's spell, readiest to talk back to him or to listen to Murray.

Coincidence?

'Hello, hello!' Roger was saying irritably. Murray came back to the here and now.

'Yes – well, that's not all. There's a girl here who apparently wasn't hired for the play at all – just to be seduced by Ida. Laid on the same way as Gerry's horse and a library of dirty books for Constant Baines. And topping the lot, as far as I'm concerned, someone – I don't see it can be anyone else except Delgado – is trying to get me back on the bottle. I don't mean pressing me openly. I mean spiking cans of fruit juice and leaving them in my room.'

'Murray, is this true?'

'Do you want to come out here and have it proved? I'd be crazy with relief if someone came and poked around and proved what I suspect. Right now, I – well, I'm doubting my own sanity half the time.'

'Hmmm . . .' from Roger.

'Roger, you're keeping something back, damn you! Spit it out. God knows, it's late enough!'

He was almost panting with impatience when Roger finally made up his mind.

'Yes, I suppose I am. I mean, I didn't credit it before, but – did I tell you why Léa Martinez wound up in the bin after the Paris production of *Trois Fois*?'

'No. You dropped some heavy hints, and I was too glad to have the offer of a decent job to pick them up. Go on.'

'She claimed that Delgado was persecuting her and trying to drive her insane. If he was, he did a damned good job. Listen, Murray – you know why I didn't spell this out to you, don't you?'

'Yes,' Murray said bitterly. 'It's something I appear to be pretty good at myself.'

'I was afraid you'd say that. So I kept my mouth shut.' Roger hesitated. 'Damn it, though, Murray! If the place is as much of a madhouse as you claim, how come Sam Blizzard – or Ida and Ade, come to that – how come everyone else is putting up with it? Is the gun supposed to be pointing just at your head and no one else's?'

'No. But –' Murray checked, biting his lip. How to explain his weird suspicions about Delgado's methods? 'Roger, I can't give you details over the phone. I'm going to try and get away. I don't know if I'll be able to –'

'*What?*'

'I'm still not kidding. The grounds are fenced all around – chain-link fencing with three strands of barbed wire – and the main gate is locked every night at eleven. I may have to leave the car and sneak out on foot.'

'Murray, I'm beginning not to believe you now.'

'Oh, Jesus!' Murray repressed an urge to throw the phone at the wall. 'Well, will this satisfy you? If I get out at all, I'll head for a doctor's place in the nearest village – I met him the other day, and he's a very reasonable guy. Make a note of him, will you? The village is called – uh – Bakesford, I think, and the doctor's name is Cromarty. Got that?'

'Yes.'

'Roger, don't think I'm quitting easily. But I think we're all set for a repeat of what happened with Delgado in Paris, and I don't want to be another Jean-Paul Garrigue.'

'Anybody would think Delgado was a reincarnation of the Marquis de Sade,' Roger said heavily. 'All right, Murray, I believe you – mostly. I know how much you wanted that job, and I guess things must have got really bad to make you cry uncle. But you realize that if you quit, you'll be in bad with Sam?'

'If Sam has to learn the hard way, by seeing his cast head one by one for jail, asylums, or cemeteries, let him. Roger, I'll try and get back to town. If I don't show up tomorrow morning, call that doctor; if he hasn't heard from me, call here, and if they refuse to pass the call or say I'm not available, then for Christ's sake come and see for yourself. Will you?'

'See what? If it was that obvious. Sam would have seen it, wouldn't he? Come off it, Murray – you're not in jail. I'll expect to see you tomorrow, but if I don't, and you're not with this doctor, I'll assume you changed your mind and decided to stick it out.'

'There's no chance of that,' Murray said earnestly. 'No chance at all.'

'Maybe not. But get this.' Roger's voice went hard. 'If you quit, and they get out a play and it's a success and nobody kills himself because of it, that'll be that, Murray. I'll be clean out of patience with you.'

'I'll take the risk,' Murray said and cradled the phone.

Talking to Roger had cleared his mind. He lit a cigarette and sat down in the chair Heather had been using. She was lying asleep on the bed now, her mouth half open. He caught up the side of the bedcover and tossed it over her, but the room was fairly warm and he wasn't concerned about the effects of what she'd drunk – she'd recover quickly in the morning.

She'd already been talking about leaving. So . . .

He was going to have to wait out the night, he decided. It was absurd to think of calling Valentine to open the main gate and carrying an unconscious girl to his car now. In the morning, then. Persuade Heather to come with him. Take whatever he could find that might serve as evidence – of what, he couldn't say, but he needed something.

Of course. The wire embroidery. He jumped out of the chair and felt for his pocket-knife. Carefully, trying not to disturb the pattern of the wires, he cut away the whole area of cloth on which it was laid out, broke the filament linking them to the tape-deck under the mattress, and rolled it up and stuffed it in his pocket.

The spool of tape, too. Why not? He held back the mattress with one hand and opened the lid over the recorder with the other. He expected to have to wind the tape back slowly by hand, but someone had been here; there was a fresh tape in position.

Oh. That figures.

He removed the spool and put it in his travelling bag. He looked wistfully at the TV set – but whatever enigma had been introduced into its vitals, it was too big to carry off. He wouldn't have much to show to back up his story.

The cans of fruit juice. He dropped them in the bag, too. And then it occurred to him that he might be able to get into Heather's room and remove her tape. That was an extra. Whatever was on the tape might prove meaningless, but it would be comforting to have solid objects he could show.

He would have to wait for his chance to sneak into Heather's room, though. Someone else might forestall him, unfortunately – Ida might come calling, and not finding her there might investigate.

Too bad. Let her.

He returned to his chair and his burning cigarette. It was bound to be a miserable wait, but it was going to have to be endured.

20

Sitting in the near silence of the house at night, Murray had the eerie sensation that he had not come of his own accord to his decisions. There seemed to be gaps in the processes of his reasoning. He could not, for instance, recall just why he had accepted the necessity of waiting till next morning before trying to get out. That had sprung itself on him. Heather's presence was part of an explanation, but it was too facile.

Gradually, he began to wonder whether in fact he lacked the courage to do as he had told Roger he would. With the passing of hours, the self-questioning grew more intense and more difficult to bear.

By one o'clock, when for over an hour there had been hardly a sound except Heather's irregular breathing nearby, he could stand it no longer. He stubbed out the latest of an endless succession of cigarettes and went cautiously to the door, intending to relieve the strain by fetching the spool of tape from Heather's room.

He opened the door fractionally and listened at the gap, wishing his blood would not rush so loudly in his ears. There was nothing to hear. He had counted doors opening and closing as the rest of the company came up to bed, had identified voices as they spoke casual good nights. He had caught Ida's faint words of inquiry at Heather's door, but she had not apparently found the answering silence remarkable; after a minute's wait she had gone to her own room and shut the door.

So unless someone woke by chance, there was little risk of his being heard.

He closed the door again and went back to see if Heather had her room-key in the pocket of her jeans. She was too deeply asleep to be disturbed by his touch. A small cigarette case; a book of matches; a handkerchief, loose change; no key. He put the bedcover back over her and left her, locking his own door very quietly from the outside.

He had just withdrawn the key when he heard the voices.

For a second, he was so startled he nearly dropped the key. Then a wave of icy control came over him, and he turned his head, locating the source of the words. They came from the room next to his – room thirteen, into which he had had no glimpse since his arrival. The door was not completely shut; he saw a thin line of light around the edge of its frame.

He unlocked his own door again, thinking of a way of retreat if someone spotted him, and then crept towards the adjacent room. So far, he had only heard an indistinct murmur, but now he began to make out words.

Hearing them was one thing. Making sense of them was another, and would have to wait till later. His jaw muscles knotted with concentration; he accepted the sounds passively.

The voices were those of Delgado and Valentine. He had not expected anyone else's. The only curious point was that Delgado's had a subservient inflection, and Valentine's was coloured with uncharacteristic authority.

'The girl isn't in her room,' Valentine said. 'The young one. What's happened to her?'

'I – I don't know.' Delgado was nervous. 'Outside, perhaps?'

'Don't be a fool. I know when anyone goes in or out. No, she's in the house.'

'Have you checked Ida's signal for a double trace?'

'She isn't there. Thanks to that interfering bastard Douglas. The urge was on her tapes four nights ago. And we haven't had a single chance to play for her.'

'We'll have to do something about Douglas,' Delgado said. 'Uh – I don't suppose she could be in his room, could she?' He brightened as the idea struck him.

'How am I supposed to know?' Valentine snapped back. 'He suspects too much. Putting the scanner into the television was a brilliant idea, you said. Nobody would suspect it, you said. Except him! I'm getting a beautiful scan of the wall of his room, and I've had nothing else all evening.'

'He doesn't *know* anything,' Delgado mumbled. 'He only has a hunch. We could deal with him by direct methods –'

'Too late,' Valentine interrupted. 'He called someone in London this evening. I listened to the call. What he doesn't *know* is hardly relevant. He's decided to leave. Moreover, he mentioned Garrigue's suicide, and the man he was talking to believed him and told him about Léa Martinez. You remember Léa?' The voice which was usually so smooth and emotionless was now a whiplash of sarcasm.

'But – nobody believed what she said! They put her in one of their primitive mental hospitals, and by now she probably really *is* out of her mind.' Delgado essayed a laugh – as it were: *this is a joke* – but it was a failure.

'Too late. He's going. You and your indirect methods! Making him think he was insane! Making him drunk by adding alcohol to his fluid intake! Well, it's too late now.'

'But he's still here, isn't he? We can use a more direct technique. It's *not* too late.' Delgado was attempting defiance now.

'Will you listen? He's told his friend he's definitely leaving, and asked him to come and make inquiries if he doesn't arrive in London tomorrow.'

'We can get around that!' Delgado insisted feverishly. 'We can make up a tape for him – fit him with convincing reasons for staying. So much the better if his friend comes here and meets him and hears why he decided to stay after all.'

'So much the better, in my view, if he goes.' Valentine spoke coldly. 'He's been a worse nuisance than Léa ever was.'

'But you don't understand!' Delgado wailed. 'What about the play? He's a leading actor in it – if he goes, probably some of the others will get disgusted and leave, and we'll be ruined!'

'The play's your worry, not mine. No!' – as though Valentine had sensed an objection rising to the other's lips. 'At the moment, I'm more concerned about that girl. She's tractable material, and I'd rather not lose her.'

'So's Douglas!' Delgado's voice was getting higher pitched. 'We got a primary tape from him his first night here and it said so – *perfectly* tractable material!'

'But we haven't been able to play to him more than once, have we?' Valentine countered bitingly. 'I said that's your worry. I want to know where the girl is. We'll do a physical check of the unscanned rooms; if she isn't there, we'll have to see if she's in Douglas's room. And if she is, heaven help you, Delgado. *That* wasn't the experience contracted for, was it?'

Murray dared wait no longer. Valentine's last statement suggested that they might emerge into the corridor any moment. He darted back to his own door, slipped inside without more than a whisper of sound, and turned the key equally silently. Then he wiped his face, astonished at the quantity of sweat greasing his skin.

What in hell were those two talking about? Unscanned rooms! Tractable material! The urge was on her tape four nights ago!

Sheer nonsense. And yet his skin crawled to remember it.

Right now, though, he had no time to wonder. He had to act quickly. He strode over to the bed and tugged at Heather's arm.

'Heather!' he whispered close to her ear. 'Wake up! For pity's sake wake up!'

She stirred a little and moaned. Oh, what could be done to wake her? He went to the washbasin and soaked a handkerchief in cold water, then put it to her face and spoke more urgently still.

'Wake up! Delgado's looking for you – you've got to hide!'

'What?' Fighting out of a mist of alcohol and natural sleep, she managed to open her eyes. 'Leave me alone, will you? I wanna *sleep*.'

'You've got to hide! Delgado's after you!'

'What?' She was coming fully awake now, and he straightened with relief. Swinging her feet to the floor, she looked blankly first at him, then at the strange room. 'Oh my God,' she said after a pause. 'I remember now. You bastard, Murray. You –'

She broke off, as though suddenly aware that she was fully dressed. One hand plucked absently at the front of her shirt as she looked down at herself.

'Listen!' Murray whispered. 'I didn't spike your drinks – do you understand? I was meant to drink them, not you. I didn't put the stuff in there. Delgado did.' Or more likely Valentine, in view of what he'd just heard, but that could wait. 'He's out looking for you. He wants you for something. You've got to *hide*.'

It was getting through at last. Wide-eyed, she stared at him. 'But – why? What's he doing, trying to make you drunk? And why should he go looking for me in the middle of the night?' She raised her left wrist and peered uncertainly at the watch on it. 'It's past one, isn't it?'

'You'll just have to take my word for the moment,' Murray pleaded. 'I don't know what he's doing, but it's thoroughly nasty, and – I'm getting the hell out in the morning, and if you take my advice you'll come too. Otherwise you'll find yourself in Ida's bed, and you won't be able to help it.'

'Ida? Goodness, I'm not going to turn Les! I didn't come to ask you whether I should or not – I wanted to know how to keep her out of my hair!' She was definitely getting her self-possession back now.

'I said you won't be able to help it. I don't know what Delgado can do, but it's connected with the tape recorders in the beds. I just – oh, never mind! They'll be here any moment.'

He swung around, looking for a hiding place. The only possibility seemed to be the built-in wardrobe. He opened the door and quickly pushed his hanging clothes to one side, then beckoned Heather.

'It'll have to be in here. There's nowhere else.'

She got off the bed and hesitantly came two paces towards him. Then she swallowed enormously.

'Murray, I – I can't,' she said in a faint voice. 'I'm a claustrophobe. I can't stand hiding in cupboards in the dark. I've never been able to, even when I was a kid.'

'But –'

'I can't,' she repeated desperately. 'I scream. I just can't help it. I scream.'

'Oh, no,' Murray said. He let his hands fall to his sides.

'Murray, what's so terrible?' she demanded. 'You can lock the door, can't you? I mean, they aren't secret police!'

'I don't think locks will keep them out,' Murray said feverishly. 'Well, we'll just have to face it out, I guess. And a damned peculiar conversation it'll be, too. Unless –'

He broke off. The last thing he had overheard Valentine say: *that wasn't the experience contracted for*. He didn't pretend to understand it, but it was obviously meant as a threat to Delgado.

'Unless what?' Heather said after a pause.

'Unless we give them a false idea.' Murray snapped off the one light which he had had burning. 'Don't argue, for God's sake. Get your clothes off – at least your jeans and panties. Put them on that chair, in plain sight from the door.' He made for the bed as he spoke, stripping off the cover and replacing the bottom sheet and pillows to hide the damage he had done to the mattress.

'Murray,' Heather said in a faint voice.

'I won't rape you!' Murray whispered savagely. 'I overheard Delgado saying something which suggested he wants you in bed with Ida and no one else. I know it's crazy – so's the whole damned business. It'll at least give him something to worry about. Oh, *please*!'

The vehemence of the last word seemed to tip the balance. With furious rapidity she unbuttoned her shirt, unzipped her jeans, kicked off her shoes. She hesitated there, then realized the room was almost totally dark, and put her underwear on the chair with the rest. The bed creaked very faintly as she scrambled in.

Murray threw his sweater and trousers on the end of the bed, shoes on the floor nearby, socks, tie and shirt on the chair with Heather's clothes. He went around the bed and got in on the far side. His foot brushed hers, and she flinched and snatched it away.

'Lie down,' he whispered. 'If they come to the door, pretend for all you're worth that you're asleep. Listen! I think I hear them coming now.'

Very faint in the silent house, there was a noise of stairs creaking. Murray rolled over into his usual sleeping position, hoping against hope that he remembered how to act deep slumber convincingly.

The footsteps came closer. They entered the corridor of the new wing. Suddenly, Heather moved towards him, putting her leg over his and nuzzling her face into his neck; he felt her skin smooth and warm against him. The very picture of satisfied lovers, they waited for the door to be opened.

21

Murray had left the key in the lock, with a vague idea of foiling a pass-key. Clearly the intruders had more sophisticated means of opening doors. There was the faintest of snicks as the wards turned; then the hushing of the bottom of the door on the thick-piled carpet; then cautious footsteps. There was no light. Murray opened one eyelid invisibly close to the pillow, and saw darkness as complete as before: there was not even a light on in the corridor now.

Apart from their cat-soft tread, the only sound from Valentine and Delgado was a hissing intake of breath when they came close to the bed.

Not the experience contracted for.

Whatever that might mean, Murray thought grimly, there was really no reason why he shouldn't give them another uncontracted experience. From the noise of breathing, he could tell that they had both gone around to Heather's side of the bed –

'You fool.' The words barely disturbed the air; genuine sleepers would never have been woken by them.

'But there was nothing on their tapes to suggest –!' That would be Delgado, very slightly louder, almost babbling.

'How could there be? We haven't had a tape from either

of them – except in the theatre – since the first night! Out of here now, quickly.'

Murray moved.

He had spent the past several moments calculating in his mind's eye exact distances and directions. When he slid out of bed, he was closer to the half-open door than either Delgado or Valentine. He was at the door while they were still dumbfounded, shut it and turned the key and put on the light within the space of a few heartbeats.

In the bed, Heather rolled over and gave a convincing pantomime of waking from deep sleep. Her intention to feign astonishment at the intrusion gave way to real surprise when she opened her eyes and saw what Murray had already seen.

Delgado and Valentine were masked. At least, that was the first impression; the upper parts of their faces were covered by black goggles with large flat lenses, and in the middle of their foreheads another lens suggested a third eye. Murray had never seen such equipment before, but he could make an excellent guess at its function. These were exceedingly compact night-vision glasses, with their own black-light sources built in.

In Valentine's left hand there was an object much harder to identify – a box, about six inches square by ten deep, held by a handle attached to one side and having on the side opposite the handle a square open-meshed grille. Whatever it was, Valentine was alarmed at it being seen, and as soon as he recovered from his first shock, he thrust it as well as he could inside his jacket.

'All right,' Murray said after a pause. 'What the devil are you doing in my room?'

Delgado's self-possession had deserted him completely; he scarcely resembled the arrogant dominating person Murray had known. By contrast, Valentine summed the situation up almost at once. He made no attempt to excuse his presence or prevaricate.

'Delgado!' he said sharply. 'You've observed him – what's he most likely to do?'

'Uh –' Delgado strove to master himself, raising a hand to peel off his dark-vision goggles. There was a sucking noise as they parted from his skin. 'Call – uh – call the others to witness the fact that we're in here, I guess.'

'How many intractables are left?'

'Stop this nonsense!' Murray interrupted harshly. He had an uneasy feeling that he knew too little, and his temporary control of events was slipping away. 'Heather, I think Delgado has a good idea. Here!' He reached behind him without taking his eyes off the intruders, unhooked a dressing-gown from the back of the door, and tossed it towards her. 'Go and wake Sam Blizzard and get him along here. Do you know which is his room?'

'Y-yes,' Heather whispered, sitting up in bed and pulling the robe around her.

There was no hint of a reaction from Valentine to tell Murray whether his guess about Blizzard's 'tractability' was right or not. But judging by the way the producer had made Delgado eat crow over scrapping the play he should be a tough customer to argue with.

Heather padded barefoot from the room. Warily, Murray concentrated on seeing that neither Valentine nor Delgado tried to make a break. But they seemed resigned to their predicament, and that nettled him.

'What's the long silence for?' he taunted. 'Thinking up a good story?'

Valentine glanced at Delgado. For public consumption, Murray guessed, he wanted to return to his former subordinate's role. Delgado, however, was too upset to take his cue, and failed to reply.

'Not enjoying this experience, hey?' Murray went on after a pause. 'Didn't you contract for it?'

Even Valentine's composure fractured at that; as for Delgado, his jaw dropped as though he had seen a ghost. 'What did you say?' he blurted.

'Quiet!' Valentine rapped.

'Ah! Beginning to get worried, are you? I'm delighted.' Murray cast around in his mind for something else that might disturb Valentine, and settled on the first possibility to strike him. 'What did you think you'd got when you hired me – another Jean-Paul Garrigue? Well, you were wrong. You got another Léa Martinez instead – with teeth this time.'

Valentine flinched visibly, and Delgado caught at his arm. 'We've got to shut him up!' he exclaimed. 'We can't let him talk like this to –'

'Hold your tongue!' Valentine snapped. 'That's exactly what he wants you to do – tell him more than he actually knows. He doesn't know anything. He can't possibly.'

'No?' Murray said, curling his lip. 'I suppose it was because I didn't know anything that I avoided all the tapes you put in my bed – and turned the television set around so my room couldn't be scanned!'

Delgado whimpered.

'Keep your head,' Valentine adjured him through white lips. 'He's bluffing. He's got a few hints and he's trying to make us think he knows it all.'

That was so true Murray almost allowed himself to smile. He repressed the impulse, wondering why it was taking Heather so long to wake Blizzard and come back.

'Your trouble's obvious, Valentine,' he said, to keep the others' minds occupied during the interminable waiting. 'You don't know anything about me. You're too used to your scanners and tapes and God knows what, and because I've been dodging I'm a mystery to you. But I don't need to use anything except my common sense. I've never become dependent on anything else. Delgado kidded Sam Blizzard along pretty well, but he didn't kid me. He lets it be seen much too easily that he doesn't care a hoot in hell about this play he's alleged to be writing with us. All he's interested in is corrupting people.'

'You don't count taking young girls to bed as corrupting them?' Valentine suggested, with a hint of sarcasm.

'I didn't have time to corrupt her, Valentine. I laid on a little trap for you, and you fell into it beautifully.' Murray smiled. It felt – and probably looked – more like a sneer.

There was a tap at the door behind him. The tension diminished sharply.

'Right!' Murray said. 'Now's your chance to explain yourselves.' He turned the handle. 'Come in, Heather!'

She complied. But not willingly. The image of her being followed by Blizzard was so imprinted on Murray's mind that for a long moment he failed to see – from the corner of his eyes – what was really happening to her.

When he did, he was so shaken that his attention left Valentine, and Valentine seized his chance. Murray had no idea what he used – possibly the heavy box he had been hiding in his coat – but he made the blow violent.

One second, Murray was turning to see Heather pinioned by another of the black-garbed 'stewards' – the tallest of the three, whose name he had never learned – both arms locked behind her back with one hand and the other clamped over her mouth, thumb and fore-finger beside her nose to choke off her breath if she dared to make a sound. The next, he was lost in a blinding aura of pain, which began at the top of his head and ended when the floor came spiralling to meet him.

He lost consciousness for perhaps a minute. When he came to, he had no energy to rise. All his willpower had been sapped by the blow and the pain. He heard voices as though they were lights in swirling fog.

'I was servicing Blizzard's tape.' That was the tall 'steward'. 'A beautiful clean record. I'd just changed it for the new playback when the girl came to the door. I imitated Blizzard's voice and took her in. She said what she wanted before I opened the door, and in view of that I brought her around.'

'Very quick thinking, Walter.' That was Valentine. 'You saved us a great deal of trouble.'

'But what are we going to do?' That was Delgado, still not recovered from his shock and dismay. 'You told me yourself, Valentine – Douglas promised his friend he was going to leave in the morning!'

'I know.' Valentine sounded impatient. 'And I no longer think we can afford to let him go so easily. I told you he was bluffing, and he was – but he was building that bluff on too many hard facts for my liking. We shall have to find out how he picked up all his clues. Walter, is everything else in order?'

'Yes, as far as I know. I'd just started the tape for Blizzard when I was interrupted, and that was the only exchange required tonight, wasn't it?'

'Yes. But it's no longer so urgent. We've overlooked something in Blizzard's case, that's certain, from the way he spoke to Manuel about the play. We can live with that for a day or two, though. Right now – Manuel!'

'Yes?' – hesitantly from Delgado.

'Go and edit up a concentrape for the girl. Put in a basic wipe at the beginning to cure her of this damned habit of cutting the triplem to her recorder. Walter, get her something to make her sleep. I want the last four nights' urges in her mind – solidly in – by morning. Is that clear?'

'It's risky, isn't it?' Walter countered. 'You might unstable her whole personality.'

'It doesn't have to hold for long. And we have bigger fish to fry, anyway. As soon as I've made my rounds, Manuel, I'll come in and help you edit a tape for Douglas. It'll have to be mainly basic wipes tonight, I'm afraid – with some kind of excuse for his deciding to stay here, of course. I doubt if this friend of his will actually come to see him, but he just possibly might. I'll think up a good way of phrasing it. Go on, out with you.'

There was the sound of the door opening and closing. Lying face down on the carpet, Murray fought to make sense of what he was hearing, and failed. Concentrape – triplem – they were without meaning for him. The only fact which he had secured was equally absurd: it was that these men were talking as if they could make adjustments to a human brain as easily as a mechanic could re-time an engine.

'What exactly happened?' Walter inquired as the door closed behind Delgado.

Valentine recounted the events of the past hour briefly. In conclusion, he said, 'But as you probably gathered from what I told Manuel, somebody's been careless. Douglas wasn't just flapping his lips when he challenged us. He's got hold of a few phrases – contracting for an experience, that's one – which just oughtn't to be in his vocabulary. Cleaning his mind will be the devil's own job. I shall have to probe for all kinds of chance references. . . . Well, it has to be done, if we aren't to abandon this project entirely. Help me to get him up on the bed. I suppose he's played his usual trick of stripping the triplem off the mattress. Never mind – I have the conditioner with me, and it may still be working after I used it to bang him on the head.'

Murray summoned up what power to act was left him by the blinding pain in his skull, and snatched at the only thing to come within reach as the two men bent to take his legs and drag him towards the bed. He put his remaining strength into a convulsive jerk, and something gave.

'Damn. I thought he was unconscious,' he heard Valentine say calmly. 'Surprising endurance they have, considering their primitive physical maintenance, don't you think?'

A foot came down cruelly on the fingers grasping the – the – what had he taken hold of, anyway? Murray saw foggily that it was the cable running from the television set into room thirteen. He hoped he had done some more damage by hauling on it. He couldn't really accept the idea, but if what Valentine had said was a guide, it might be his last act of his own volition before they turned him into a puppet.

'Just a second,' he heard Walter say. 'He hasn't stopped at stripping off the triplem tonight. He's removed the tape as well.'

'Probably thrown it out of the window again,' Valentine sighed. 'Go and get a fresh spool from Manuel, will you? I shall have to have a fairly long recording of Douglas before I can make up his wipes.'

'Right.' Walter moved towards the door.

Painfully, Murray gathered the tattered shreds of his faculties. If he could even get to his feet while Valentine was alone in the room –

'Is something wrong?' Valentine said sharply.

'Yes,' Walter snapped. 'I smell something. I think it's burning.'

'A fire?' Valentine started. 'Look in thirteen, quick!'

Noise of a door opening. A cry of alarm. 'It's an inferno in there! He must have caused an arc when he pulled that cable! I told Manuel –'

'Never mind! Get Victor! Run for it – these places were built like tinderboxes!'

'What about – ?'

'The rest of them can take their chance! *I'm* not going to stay and be roasted alive! Out of my way, damn you!'

22

It reached Murray's nostrils then – the acrid scent of burning rubber. It galvanized him and drove him unsteadily to his feet. The room swam; he struggled to fix the blurs of colour into images of actual objects.

The first thing he saw clearly was Heather, dumped in the easy chair. A sleeve had been torn out of the gown she wore and used to gag her. It was patched dark with saliva in front of her mouth. Her eyes were wide and rolling. Her arms had been bound with the sash of the gown, and her ankles with Murray's tie.

When he did not move directly towards her, she moaned and tried to draw his attention. But he had gone to the bed to find his pocket-knife in his trousers. Fumbling it open, he bent and slashed her bonds.

'Go and wake the others!' he ordered harshly. 'Don't stop to get your clothes on. *Hurry!*'

She paused only long enough to thrust her feet into her shoes. Then, clutching the dressing gown around her, she fled from the room.

Alone, Murray stumbled to the washbasin and cupped up cold water to pour over his aching head. The treatment was without effect; his skull went on ringing like a gong. Striving to plan rationally despite the waves of pain, he spoke aloud to himself as he swayed before his reflection in the mirror above the basin.

'Something to prove the truth. Take something with me. The tape, at least. Or the box Valentine left behind, the one he hit me with – *Christ!*'

Without thinking what he was doing, he had put his hand on the wall beside him for support, and it had taken long seconds for the report of his nerves to sink in.

That wall was hot! And beyond it was room thirteen, and Delgado!

Everything else vanished from his mind. He dashed into the corridor. Tearful, Heather confronted him, forgetting her loose gown as she caught his arm.

'Murray, I can't wake anybody! They're like – like vampires lying in their beds!'

'Try again! Try harder! If you can't manage it I'll help you drop them out of the window – they're not going to have a chance in this!'

He pointed to the door of room thirteen. It was closed, but fumes were leaking from the keyhole and between the door and the carpet.

'Delgado's still in there! Valentine and his precious friends have run off and we may never catch them – but if we can hang on to Delgado we've got one man who can answer our questions!'

He brushed her aside and flung open the door of the blazing room.

Walter's guess had probably been pretty accurate. There was no shortage of power to cause an arc when the cable was broken. It filled the air with a stink of ozone even though there were flames licking up at a dozen places. A brilliant cascade of sparks was continuing somewhere under the window. Something exploded as he flung wide the door, and he ducked instinctively. Hot fragments of glass peppered his forehead and limbs. He was wearing nothing but jockey shorts and a singlet and the heat struck at his skin as though a furnace door had been slid back.

He had no time to examine what the mysterious room held. He had received only a vague impression of banks of complex electronic equipment across which flames and arcing sparks vied to outdo one another in brightness before he saw the limp body of Manuel Delgado slumped over what might have been a vastly elaborate tape-mixing panel.

Murray plunged forward, smoke and fumes stinging his eyes. Something that bit like a venomous snake sent a jab into his heel – a red-hot fragment on the floor, perhaps. He caught Delgado by one arm and one leg and somehow got him on his shoulders. As he turned back to the door, there was a second explosion, and the floor lurched under him. He stumbled out of the room, remembering somewhere in the back of his muddled mind that opening doors was bad because it let oxygen get to the fire. He slammed the door behind him.

In the same split second as the slam, a third and this time vast explosion rent the air. A jolt travelled up his arm, numbing it. A dreadful crackling sound like a bonfire a hundred times magnified followed the explosion.

'Murray!'

From another room – Ida's, he thought – Heather emerged, ghost-pale with terror, and stumbled towards him.

'Murray, I can't wake *anybody*! I've shouted and slapped and – and – oh God, Murray, I *can't*!'

'Get down in the hall,' Murray ordered savagely, forcing his unwilling feet towards the landing in the main building. 'Find a phone. Call the fire brigade, then ambulances and doctors, then the police. Make sure they *all* come. This wing is bound to go first, but the rest of the house will last for a while.'

He came now to the landing, and at the head of the stairs bent to spill his unconscious burden down them. Delgado fell like a dummy, coming to rest against the balusters at the first curve.

He'd live, Murray decided cynically. If he was alive at the moment. Part of his hair had been scorched away, and a charred sleeve and trouser leg suggested probable burns, but nothing beyond a doctor's capacity to treat.

'Get to that phone!' he added with violence, and didn't stop to see if Heather obeyed before diving back along the landing of the rear wing.

There followed an appalling period which he never remembered clearly. It was compounded of nightmare, pain, and a prevision of hell. It began in room twelve where Adrian Gardner lay wax-white in his bed as though – Heather's phrase – he were a true vampire, one of the undead. No wonder Valentine and Delgado had grown careless and left the door of room thirteen ajar while they discussed their secrets together!

If they were sure that most of the other people in the house were locked in this corpse-like slumber, they would naturally grow over-confident.

He entered Adrian's room with a half-formulated plan to strip off the – what was the word? – the triplem from the mattress and perhaps throw the spools of tape out to be retrieved later from the garden. That intention died the moment he set foot inside the door. Already fumes were winding up from the skirting, and the air smelled pungently of burning. The monstrous crackling, just beyond the wall, was immensely loud.

He ripped back the covers from the bed and struggled to raise Ade in the same not-quite fireman's lift he had used to get Delgado to the stairs. Something shorted in room thirteen. The TV set in here exploded, showering bits of glass from its cathode tube all over the place. Smoke rose from the cable; after a moment, flames followed, jetting from the point in the floor where that cable presumably disappeared like the one in his own room.

Gasping, he carried Ade to the door. Behind him the carpet smouldered and began to flare up, adding the unpleasant stench of burning acetate to the already burdened air. The door of room thirteen was showing blisters as the paint on it lifted with the heat behind.

He was returning from dumping Ade as he had dumped Delgado – his original intention of carrying the others down to the hall forestalled – when the whole upper floor of the new wing seemed to tremble under him. Something roared and crashed, and Murray pictured all that immensely heavy equipment in room thirteen plunging down into the auditorium of the theatre – no, on to the stage, which was worse yet, with all its inflammable hangings! Once a fire got a hold down there, he would be separated only by floorboards, joists, and a plaster shell of a ceiling from a real furnace. Frantically he tried to open the next room – number eleven, Constant's.

The damned fool had locked his door.

He spun around, seeking a tool to break it down; he knew he could not charge it with enough force to smash the lock. His eye fell on a heavy wooden chair. With that as a kind of crude hammer, he managed to shatter the panels of the door –

luckily, it was a modern type made of hardboard stretched over a timber frame.

By the time he had dragged – not carried; he was too weak – Gerry from room ten, there was no question of the fire having taken a hold in the theatre. The floor was distinctly hot under him, and smoke was wreathing up everywhere. The door of room thirteen had broken open in flames some time in the recent past, and the carpet was lifting like dry paper. He heard windows shatter with a cascade of tinkling glass, and dared not spend even a second in wondering which windows. Smoke billowed around him. The floor shifted a second time and then settled at an acute angle. Or was that an illusion due to his weariness? For the angle seemed to be making a slope against him whichever way he happened to be going, to or from the head of the stairs –

'Thank you,' he muttered, and realized he had spoken aloud and that there was someone to hear him: Heather, her robe in forgotten shreds, helping him carry Ida, wax-white, in a black, filmy nylon nightdress, as the others had been carried . . . funny, one would have thought Ida would wear rather masculine pyjamas in view of . . . look out, something must have happened in this room, maybe fire attacking from under the floor because the edge of the bed-cover . . .

Choking, eyes streaming, on feet so painful they had to be forgotten or they would have insisted on rest, Murray and Heather somehow cleared the new wing, which was worst threatened by the fire. The stairs looked like a set for a modern-dress *Hamlet*, with corpses littering it . . .

'Sam now!' Hand clutching at him. Yes, one more, not in the vulnerable new wing over the hollow blaze of the theatre but in the older part of the house and less endangered.

'All right, all right –' But that wasn't Heather he was talking to now. A figure in dark clothes, with bright buttons. Someone with a helmet.

'I told them to send all the fire brigades in the neighbourhood and the doctors and –'

That was Heather. Murray paused, looking around him. Past the limp Dali-dolls on the stairs, men dragging tails of canvas hose, someone shouting orders, a question: *is everyone out of there*?

Heather's voice again: 'He got them out. Murray got them out. Yes, they're all safe!'

Firemen. Hoses. Noise of windows being smashed, not just breaking under the heat. Hope. Help.

Murray forgot everything. He clutched at the balusters of the staircase, missed his hold, saw the huge hall swing through a quarter-circle and felt his right foot tread on air where he had meant there to be solidity. Someone snatched at him as he passed, caught his shoulder. He looked into a serious, concerned, strange face under a black sloping helmet.

Fireman.

Murray fainted.

23

Painful as the travail of birth, inexorable as the accretion of planets – and seemingly as slow: the fragments of Murray Douglas' awareness drifted back from the limitless nowhere into which they had scattered. After he had regained consciousness, he was content to stay as he was for long moments, feeling the rough warmth of a blanket around him, the softness of a roll of cloth under his head, and hearing the confusion of noises in which were mingled shouts, the roar of engines and the crackle of flames.

Then someone near him said anxiously, 'Here he is, Doctor. He – he just passed out.'

Heather's voice.

Another, gruffer, with a trace of Scots accent: 'I'm not surprised, young woman! I saw him the other day and I was shocked, really shocked, to see how much older he looked than his chronological age.'

Doctor ... Dr Cromarty. The name moved sluggishly to the forefront of Murray's mind, and he forced open his eyes. There was the doctor before him, the collar of a striped pyjama jacket showing above the neck of the sweater he had pulled on when he was called from bed.

Murray said, 'Are they all right? Did we get them all out?'

In the act of putting on his glasses to commence his examination, Cromarty blinked rapidly several times. 'Yes, Mr Douglas, the others are all right. Now you just lie still there and let me –'

'I don't mean were they *burned*?' Murray interrupted. He struggled to get his elbows behind him and force his body off the ground where he was lying. 'I mean *are they all right*?'

Cromarty made hushing noises and tried to persuade him to lie flat again. Murray pushed him aside impatiently. 'For God's sake!' he exploded. 'I'm okay – I only passed out from the smoke and the heat. I –'

'Your feet,' Heather whispered. He paused, momentarily at a loss; then he realized she was right and the soles of both his feet indeed felt tender. Nonetheless, the pain was bearable, and so it wasn't urgent. What counted was those undead he had carried from their beds, pallid and waxy as corpses, victims of whatever evil scheme Delgado and his accomplices had woven around them.

'The *hell* with me,' he grunted, and this time succeeded in ridding himself of Cromarty's restraining hands. He scrambled up, the blanket falling in a heap. 'I want to know . . .'

The words trailed away as he took in the scene. He was not the only casualty to have been laid on this grass verge fringing the drive of Fieldfare House. The headlights of two fire engines and several cars – including his own, which had been pushed away from the house to make a clear way for the fire-fighters – showed him a ghastly rank of bodies, like an open-air mortuary. Dark-uniformed men were everywhere coming and going.

'Get that trailer-pump over to the swimming-pool!' yelled a high excited voice, and then, almost cutting off the last word, there was a rending crash behind the house. Murray jerked his head around and saw a fountain of sparks, bright as a firework, spatter the underside of the pall of stinking smoke now smearing across the sky.

Whatever the key is to this mystery, we won't find it where the fire has taken hold . . .

He closed his eyes for a few seconds, drawing on every

ounce of self-control. When the crash startled him, he had been about to ask a bewildered question. He fought back to it, remembered what it was, and turned to meet Dr Cromarty's concerned gaze.

'Ambulances,' he said. 'Why aren't there any ambulances here?'

'There's been an accident on the motorway,' the doctor muttered. 'Sixty people hurt in a long-distance bus. But they promised to come as soon as they could.'

'Oh, *Jesus*,' Murray said with jolting dismay. 'Well, then – have you looked these people over yet?'

'Ah –' Cromarty wiped his face. 'I only got here a moment ago, I'm afraid. The firemen are trained in first aid, of course, and when they assured me there were no serious burn cases, this young lady insisted I come to examine you because you –'

'Delgado?' Murray rapped.

'They told me he'd had an electric shock,' Heather said. 'But he's not badly hurt and ought to be all right.'

Relieved, Murray swung back to his earlier demand. 'Doctor, what's wrong with these people? They aren't asleep. They're like vampires. They – hell, don't let me just talk about them! See for yourself!'

He took the four or five strides needed to bring him level with the nearest of the 'undead', and found on the last step that his feet were far worse hurt than he had imagined. He swayed with the stab of pain, and Heather was beside him, putting her arm around to steady him. Cromarty followed, opening his surgical bag one-handed and reaching into it.

'Here, young woman!' he rapped, offering a large jar of salve and a packet of dressings. 'Sit this idiot down on the grass, and put some of that on his burns before he gets dirt in them! I'll clean him up properly later, but at least this will ease the pain.'

Heather accepted the medicaments silently and helped Murray to sit, then fetched his blanket and wrapped it around his shoulders. Her ministrations were quick and gentle; they hardly distracted Murray from his concentrated staring after Cromarty.

The elderly doctor went down the line of bodies one by

one, pausing beside each. Finally he returned to Murray, his face pale and drawn.

'I don't know what to make of this,' he said. 'But I'm sure of one thing. When you said they weren't sleeping, you were half right. Those poor folk are in a hypnotic trance.'

'Are you certain?' Murray demanded.

'Absolutely.' Cromarty gave a bashful cough. 'My practice here is not the most time-consuming in the world, and I've been able to keep up an interest I've had ever since I was a student in the medical applications of hypnosis. I've used it for many painless deliveries hereabouts, when I could gain the consent of the mother.'

'I thought –' Heather, pausing in her application of salve to Murray's burns, bit her lip.

'Yes?'

'Well. . . . Might they not be drugged?'

'There's one young man who exhibits the symptoms of heroin addiction, or I'm an ignoramus,' Cromarty said. 'But that's not significant. I'd stake my reputation on their being in trance.'

'Can you get them out of it?' Murray exclaimed.

The doctor shook his greying head. 'If the induction was skilfully done, they will respond only to a particular stimulus.'

'They'll stay like that indefinitely?' Heather cried.

'Oh no!' Cromarty looked shocked. 'Eventually the trance will merge into normal sleep, and they'll wake of their own accord. But –'

'Yes?' Murray prompted.

'But there may have been post-hypnotic commands,' Cromarty said slowly. 'And unless we can find out what they were the poor folk will carry them out willy-nilly when they wake.'

Murray had seen stage demonstrations of hypnosis often enough before they were regulated by law to realize the implications of Cromarty's statement. Failure to erase hypnotic commands could lead to behaviour that appeared insane.

Before he could speak again, another car braked sharply at the entrance to the driveway, and a man in police uniform jumped out and held the door for another in a tweed jacket.

This latter, after brief words with a police constable already present, looked around, recognized Cromarty, and approached him briskly.

'Morning, doctor!' he said. 'Sorry I'm so late on the scene, but they picked the very devil of a night to have this fire here.'

'When do we get some ambulances?' Cromarty demanded.

'Thirteen of the bloody things it took to clear up after our coach-crash – you know about that? But we passed messages to the various hospitals to send a few along as soon as they've unloaded.... What in the world is going on here, anyhow?'

'I was just about to ask Mr Douglas here the same thing.' Cromarty said with a touch of grimness. 'Mr Douglas – Chief Inspector Wadeward of the County Constabulary.'

'Murray Douglas,' the chief inspector nodded. 'I heard you were with the company rehearsing here. Saw you in *Skeleton* a few years ago – a very fine performance you gave... Well?'

Murray licked his lips. Heather had finished her work with a professionally knotted bandage around each of his feet, and was sitting back on her heels gazing up curiously, too exhausted to rise.

'The whole thing is so complicated I hardly know where to begin,' Murray prevaricated, trying to order his thoughts.

'You could begin with the reason why all these people are hypnotized,' Cromarty growled.

'Did you say hypnotized?' Wadeward turned incredulously to glance along the prostrate forms on the grass. 'I – no, give me some background before I start asking questions, for pity's sake!'

'Well, you know why we were supposed to be here?' Murray suggested.

'To work up a new play,' Wadeward said. 'It was in the local paper – quite a big event, apparently.'

'Except that that was just a cover story,' Murray broke in. 'What the real reason was, I can't be sure, but I think it had something to do with raising us to a pitch of complete hysteria. And then...'

Triplem.

Concentrape.

The experience contracted for.

No good. At this point his brain started to fill with fog as dense as the smoke now raging skyward like a thundercloud from the inferno at the back of the house.

'I – uh – I'd better go over it from the beginning,' he muttered.

With growing astonishment, Cromarty and Wadeward heard about *Trois Fois à la Fois*, the suicide of Jean-Paul Garrigue, the insanity of Léa Martinez, the attempt by Claudette Myrin to kill her baby daughter. At that point Wadeward was already finding silence impossible.

'But wasn't something done about this – this maniac?' he exploded. 'You can't just have someone persecuting innocent victims in the name of art, genius or not!'

'He's so clever you have to experience his treatment to believe it,' Murray said. 'I don't know how we escaped it – luck, I guess.'

'No, not luck,' Heather said firmly. 'You were too tough a proposition for him, Murray.'

'Flattering, but not true.' Murray sighed. 'Well, from the first evening ...'

So: the tape-decks under the beds, the gadgetry over the stage, in room thirteen, hidden in all the TV sets, Delgado's touchiness on the subject, the unwillingness even of Lester Harkham to pursue the matter after the first day or two; scraps and hints picked up from Valentine's unguarded conversation earlier tonight, about 'scanning the rooms' and 'basic wipes' and the matter of spiking canned fruit juice and framing Murray into believing he'd been drinking and – and – and ...

With a sober headshake, Wadeward confessed, 'I simply don't know what to make of it – do you, doctor? One thing I can do is put out a call for these mysterious "stewards" on suspicion of trafficking in illegal drugs, and perhaps procuring for immoral purposes too. Oh! Sorry, young lady,' he added to Heather.

'I think,' the girl said in a strained voice, not looking directly at him, 'that they'd have made me do what they wanted if Murray hadn't prevented them.'

'But the whole thing's incredible!' Cromarty objected. 'To take the most glaring example, Mr Douglas here thinks patterns of wire on their mattresses were responsible for all these people being hypnotized. But I've made a lifetime hobby of the subject, and to me it sounds absurd!'

The dogmatic certainty in his tone lay on Murray's mind like a dead weight. He made to voice counter-arguments, and decided to save his breath. Everything he had planned to use for evidence was in the wreckage of the new wing; even if a few of the items were later salvaged, what would they amount to in most people's view? Some bits of pseudo-scientific mumbo-jumbo, better fitting Lester's theory that Delgado was the dupe of charlatans than his own fantastic proposals.

He put his head in his hands. Alarmed, Cromarty bent to examine him and this time brooked no denial of his intentions. Murray submitted wanly and let his mind go so blank he barely heard Heather's next words.

'Instead of wild guessing,' she was saying to anyone who cared to listen, 'why not ask Delgado? His fall down the stairs knocked him silly, but he should have recovered by this time. Valentine and the others have probably got clear away, but Delgado's right over there.'

24

That jolted Murray from apathy to impatience. If he hadn't been so bemused, he'd have thought of it himself – he had in fact done so, then forgotten the matter of questioning the so-called 'playwright' in the all-excluding need to rescue the other members of the company.

He was almost frantic by the time Cromarty had checked the man over and confirmed that he was only slightly hurt. In this case – whatever was true of the rest of the people carried from the house – paleness was due to simple shock, and the routine administration of first aid had already brought him round before Cromarty reached him. Now, he was shivering with terror, his eyes enormous, his skin taut over his teeth so that his lips would not quite meet, and the noise of his repeated swallowing was so loud it could be heard over the racket of the firefighting.

On Cromarty's nod of permission, Wadeward dropped to one knee beside him and identified himself, then demanded an explanation of the story Murray had told.

The only response was a terrified moan and another attempt to make his lips close.

'Bastard!' Murray thundered at him. 'Talk, damn you! Talk!'

He was so furious he would have kicked the prostrate man, had a pang from his burned sole not prevented him. Cromarty was preoccupied and hadn't noticed Murray walking on the bandages, or he would doubtless have ordered him to lie down again.

'It's no good keeping quiet,' Heather said suddenly. 'It won't help you. They left you to die – don't you realize that?'

A spark of interest. The terror subsided for an instant and Delgado cocked his head, eyes on her face.

'They left you to die in room thirteen,' Heather insisted. 'Valentine, and – and Victor, and Walter! We don't know where they are, but they said they weren't going to stay and be roasted alive. They ran away and left you, and if it hadn't been for Murray *you'd* have been burned alive. Don't you understand? Your bloody stinking friends left you to burn, and Murray saved your worthless dirty horrible disgusting *life*!'

She was almost crying from the intensity of her emotion when she reached the last word. It broke through Delgado's armour of fear and naked hatred showed in his grimace.

'Is that true?' he whispered, and didn't wait for the answer. 'Yes – yes, I remember! I was going to make up that tape Valentine wanted, and then there was a – a shock, and something sparked, and I touched the console and –'

He forced himself abruptly into a sitting position and stared wildly in all directions. His darting gaze settled finally on Murray's face.

'You – brought me out of there?' he croaked.

Murray gave a dispirited nod.

'But I thought ...' He lasped into silence, and when he spoke again the anger in his voice was so feral it was frightening to hear it from such a small man, as though one called kitty – kitty! and in response a tiger came purring through the night.

'Those dirty perverted mother-loving sons of radiated ova. Those heartless gutless sewer-brained sadists. Left me. To burn.' The words were as level as a machine's, but they blazed with his rage. 'Then I'll leave them something. Let them try and explain this away when the temporegs get hold of them. Let them just try. I'll bury them to their necks in radiating garbage. I'll have them wiped till they can't do more than drool pabulum down their chins. I'll have them blanked into substates and forbidden redukes. I'll –'

Substates? Redukes? Triplem? Concentrape? Murray leaned forward and spoke harshly.

'Save your breath. They can't hear you. What's triplem, Delgado?'

The playwright closed his eyes, leaning back on his elbows and letting his body go slack in absolute resignation to his fate.

'Triplem? That's micro-miniaturized multicore cable. The stuff you kept tearing off your mattress. You wouldn't have recognized it – it won't be developed until 1989.'

There was an instant of absolute discontinuity. At first Murray was able to believe he hadn't heard correctly – there was, after all, so much row coming from the fire fighters around the house . . .

Then it dropped into place. He had heard right, and it fitted. By God, it fitted *exactly*. Incredible or not, it made everything into a sensible pattern. So far he was only groping after it, but that one clue made him feel he was on the trail of a solution instead of a multitude of baffling questions.

He said very slowly, 'And – temporegs? I think that's what you called them.'

'Temporal regulators,' muttered Delgado. 'A sort of police. And when they catch up with Valentine I hope they –'

'Substate?' Murray snapped, leaning forward.

'An incorrigible adult criminal who's had his personality wiped because he's too far gone for psychotherapy.'

'Redukes?'

'Re-educational tapes, used to impress a social personality in place of a criminal one.'

'Concentrape?' Murray glanced around his other listeners; Cromarty and Wadeward were completely bewildered, but Heather was hanging on his every word with shining eyes.

'An illegal tape prepared in order to shift the foundations of someone's existing personality towards another desired orientation.' Delgado's answers were recited tonelessly, as a child might mouth a poem memorized but not understood.

'Conditioner?' That was the box Valentine had hit him on the head with.

'A device giving temporary but absolute control over the actions of someone else.'

'Does this – this conditioner produce a state resembling a hypnotic trance?'

'It *is* a hypnotic trance.'

Right. Murray drew a deep breath. 'Manuel Delgado, when were you born?'

'Now just a moment,' Wadeward said, starting forward. 'I don't follow the –'

'Shut up!' Murray blazed, and repeated his question. There was a tense pause. Finally Delgado licked his lips.

'After what I've told you already – and I hope it's enough to sterilize Valentine and make his hair fall out and his gums bleed and –'

'Delgado!'

'Oh ... I was born in year 218 of the World Calendar. By your primitive measurement that would be – uh – about 2429.'

Murray rocked back very gently on his heels. He said, 'Then I can tell you what you've been doing here. You've been bootlegging experiences.'

Delgado jerked like a frog's leg connected to a battery. He said, 'Now I'm not going to –'

'You *are*,' Murray contradicted firmly. 'You're not going to get away with breaking the letter of your – your temporal regulations. You're going to smash a hole in them so wide you could take one of our *primitive* motorcars through it – hear me?'

'But I can't!' Delgado wailed. 'I mustn't! I –'

Murray loomed over him, projecting with all the force at his command, knowing that this was the performance of his career, with infinitely more at stake than favourable notices and a long run. He said, 'Delgado! If you don't tell us the whole truth, I shall pick you up and carry you into that house and put you back where I found you, and not all your futuristic gadgetry will stop me.'

He closed his hand on a fistful of Delgado's shirt. At the corner of his eye he saw Wadeward framing an interruption, Heather laying a pleading hand to restrain him, Cromarty tapping his glasses on his palm with an air of fascinated incomprehension.

'But you don't understand!' babbled Delgado. 'If I tell you any more, the things they'll do to me –'

'Wipe you?' Murray snorted contemptuously. 'It'll be an improvement, that's certain! Clean out the dirty corners of that mind of yours! But they aren't here, are they? And I am! Well, which is it to be – do you talk, or do you go back into that blazing house and roast like a leg of pork?'

'But if I talk, then I . . .' Delgado's voice faded below audibility. Then he seemed to take a fresh grip on himself.

'Well, what's the alternative? There's nothing to hope for, is there? Stuck here – damn Valentine! – among these stinking backward idiots. If I keep my mouth shut they'll probably lock me in one of their horrible mental asylums like that girl in Paris – I couldn't stand that, and at least this is a quick way out . . .'

'A quick way out?' Murray echoed, tightening his grasp on the other's shirt. 'Doc, you'd better make sure he hasn't got a suicide pill!'

Cromarty exclaimed and stepped forward, but Delgado waved him aside with a gesture of arrogant superiority.

'Poison? Is that what you mean? Oh, I'm not that far deviant – if I'd had suicidal tendencies they'd have wiped them while I was an adolescent. I'm not a self-killer. I'm simply a condemned man.'

He returned his gaze to Murray, and a spark of unaccountable glee flickered behind his sinister eyes.

'Executioner,' he said softly. 'Well, ask away. But I make no promises as to how many questions will get answers.'

'All of them,' Murray threatened, 'or I carry you back in that house as I promised. After the things you've tried to do to me –'

'If you want revenge,' Delgado sneered, 'you'll get it in full measure, and I hope you sleep easily when you've enjoyed it. You primitives must have strong stomachs to put up with your ordinary lives, but if this is too much for you then you won't have the help I can get when I go back each time. You don't have wipes for loathsome memories – you just have to endure them, don't you?'

'Shut up,' Murray said again. His memory held too many loathsome things for him to stand this line of taunting.

'Mr Douglas,' Cromarty put in nervously, 'there's one thing I must know before you go any further. How about the others lying here? Since their condition is so – so unusual . . .'

'Leave them alone,' Delgado grunted. 'Take them to one of your insanitary bedlams or whatever you call them and let them wake up. Nothing's been done to them beyond reinforcing tendencies already there – they'll recover in a few weeks or months.' Once more he glowered at Murray. 'Thanks to this meddler here!'

Cromarty hesitated, then shrugged. He stared towards the gate, as though he could will the long-delayed ambulances to arrive.

Ignored for the moment, Delgado was running along his previous track. 'Couldn't stand it here anyway, so what the hell? Bad enough up there where there are still people who like this kind of thing for a forbidden thrill, but here they glorify it as "art" and talk about it openly and . . .'

'What?' Murray said stonily. There was no reply. After a brief wait, he persisted, 'Delgado! What are you really?'

'A – I'll get the term in a second, they gave me a good vocabulary from the records. . . . A fall guy. A stooge.' The blood had drained utterly from his face now, and he was whiter than wax. 'Didn't expect to find you so ready to accept the truth, I must say – thought anyone in this benighted century would dismiss it as impossible – but then, that was the trouble with picking you in the first place. I did tell Valentine, but catch him listening to advice!'

'Stick to the point,' Murray rapped.

'Point, yes ...' He was definitely weakening; his words declined to the level of a whisper. 'Well, then: you know we have means to visit the past, but it's dangerous and insanitary and illegal and – anyhow, we have the techniques for manipulating the mind, too, and the personality. Some people say it's the next great step forward, and some people say it's a living death because the individuals with the greatest endowment of imagination and creativity are also often the least stable, but I don't take sides in that argument. I've merely found out how much I hate the idea of having my mind made over by some official or other to conform with a socially acceptable norm – pretty soon, I guess, *you'll* see just how much, too.' He chuckled as if at some private joke, and sweat beaded his forehead.

'Now you can't wipe and reduke the whole population of ten billion-odd, so they do only criminals and voluntary asocial deviants. That leaves plenty who behave in public and misbehave in private. And the machinery you've seen is available generally and it's used for entertainment and – well, like you're separating from your girl and the last time you bed her you make tapes for each of you to be reminded by. And things ...

'But you can't get some things you want if you're a bit deviated. Talk about the healthy primitivism of the past and the sterile boredom of the modern age, and what you mean is you'd like to get drunk, or bed your own sex, or something.' The coherence of his explanation was failing fast, and Murray felt his brows drawing together in anxiety.

'So comes Valentine and tries to fill this gap by taping primitives like you – has access to a timer because he works in a plant making them, only two plants on the planet because the temporegs say you *don't* without authority. Got one, anyway. Did a dry run, this century – earliest we can empathize with the people. Didn't work. All that risk for nothing. Meaningless garble on the tapes. Tried next century up – no good either, too modern, too bland and civilized. No drunks, no dope addicts, no big-kick thrills for taping except in back corners of the world where we don't empathize the people there either.

'Me.' He licked his lips. 'Only clever idea I had in my life, originally as I was. This personality you've seen – it was taped on me. I was a mouse with ambitions when I started, and I guess that's what I'll be when I finish. Soon, soon . . .'

He winced, but waved aside Heather when she made to approach him.

'Actors, I said to Valentine. Get actors. People who live half their lives in their imaginations. Even when they're bedding each other it's half to an audience. Unstable types – alcoholic, drugged, sexually fouled up. . . . And it worked. Tried in Argentina first, made one fortune from the tapes. Ran it in Paris, made two fortunes. Three fortunes he's made out of my idea, the radiated pig, and leaves me to burn to death while he gets in the timer and runs squalling to safety. Pig, pig, *pig*!'

Cromarty would have spoken but that Wadeward hushed him.

'Trying to find out how close we can come to modern times, you see. Next, America – or maybe Sweden. But where the trends are set. China's too respectable already. But Japan I wanted to use. Yes, Japan . . .'

This time it was more than a wince that broke off the words, and Heather shuddered. Murray hesitated, not knowing if he should press the weakening man further, and into the hiatus Cromarty thrust a savage exclamation.

'That man's ill!'

His hand shot down and twitched aside the blanket in which Delgado had been wrapped against shock, and they saw what penalty he had brought on himself by telling the truth illegally, what he had referred to obliquely during his recital, what he had meant when he said they would need strong stomachs.

Specialist in cancer and gangrene . . .

Through what diabolical conditioning, through what psychosomatic technique of the future none of them could tell, his body had rotted as he talked. Under the blanket, from chest to ankles, his flesh had dissolved into a liquescent, putrid, utterly revolting slime.

In the distance, shrill and manic as the laughter of devils, there rang out the yammer of the ambulances' bells.

25

Heather's hands closed on Murray's arm so tightly the grip hurt, and she began to breathe in great sobbing gasps, as if fighting the need to vomit. Wadeward put a finger in his mouth and gnawed at the knuckles, and from all sides men hurried up, alerted by their frightened withdrawal, to stare down and stand petrified at the disgusting sight. Even Cromarty, with his years of medical experience, had to force himself to feel for a pulse before throwing the blanket over Delgado's face and turning away. He muttered something Murray barely caught; it sounded like, 'Beyond hope, thank God!'

Then the ambulances were swinging up the drive, disgorging their crews of tired and irritable men, and there was a welcome distraction for Cromarty and Wadeward to seize. Murray, though, had no such good fortune. He could only sway back and forth on the spot where he stood, the weight of Heather clinging to his arm an insupportable burden that somehow did not drag him down, and feel his mind swimming with crazy visions.

He'd been compelled to accept at face value the most fantastic nonsense he'd ever heard, and the impact of it had numbed him so that it was an eternity before he next perceived an outside event.

Then, it was Cromarty and Wadeward crossing his field of vision with stretcher-bearers following, directing that the loathsome ruin of Delgado should be lifted and carried away. He stirred and turned luck-lustre eyes on the doctor.

'Mr Douglas, you're shivering – and no wonder!' Wadeward, noticing him again. 'Man, you're practically naked! Someone get him a coat to put on!'

Don't shout, it hurts my ears. But the words wouldn't emerge.

'Doctor, are the ambulances full up?'

'Damned fools only sent us two!' Cromarty pushing spread

fingers through his hair, comb-fashion. 'But never mind, I'll take care of Mr Douglas. I have a spare bed, and I want to put a proper dressing on those burned feet, anyway. No disrespect to you, young woman. A very tidy job of bandaging. Wouldn't disown it myself.' He was talking feverishly for the sake of talking. 'But how about you? You're in rags even if you aren't hurt yourself, and – oh, you'd best come too. My car's there by the gate.'

Firm hands relieved Murray of the problem of balancing upright, provided relief for aching muscles and agonized feet, guided his arms laxly into the sleeves of a warm police overcoat. He saw that the firefighters were slacking their efforts now; the inferno would probably last till dawn or later, but it had been contained and would not engulf the rest of the building.

Hope they carried plenty of insurance. Hate to see Sam Blizzard bankrupted over this . . .

Stumbling, leaning on Cromarty and a policeman summoned by Wadeward, Murray suffered himself to be put in the back seat of the doctor's car and propped up with a blanket rolled into a sort of sausage. Heather slipped in beside him and took his hand.

Darkness, speared by the car's headlights, brought calm after the hellish glare of the fire they had left. Heather sensed the fact, and gave the hand she held a comforting caress.

Murray found a memory that spewed up at random and seemed important. He said, 'Uh – Dr Cromarty, you may have another visitor in the morning. My agent, Roger Grady. I said on the phone to him last night I was going to try and get away if I could and make for your place.'

Last night? This same interval between day and day? God, how short can eternity be?

'Wish I had my pipe,' the doctor muttered. 'Dragged me out in such a panic I didn't bring anything except the car keys and my surgical bag. . . . Sorry, Mr Douglas?' He half-turned his head, swinging the car around a curve. 'My mind was wandering.' Then, hearing what had been said in memory: 'Try to get away? Man, you sound as if you were in a concentration camp!'

'It was like that,' Heather said clearly. 'Didn't you follow what Murray was saying?'

'I – uh – I can hardly credit it,' Cromarty admitted. 'No disrespect, Mr Douglas, but you're overwrought and –' He interrupted himself. 'No, by the lord Harry! I do believe it, every word, now I've seen that impossible dissolution. It's like the story by Poe, isn't it?'

'*Monsieur Valdemar,*' Heather said. Murray felt a shudder run through her and heard her teeth chatter briefly. She added, 'He was hypnotized, wasn't he? Doctor, there's no risk, is there, that all the others will –?'

'You heard Delgado himself say they'd wake up naturally and recover in a few weeks or months,' Murray reminded her, and put his arm around her shaking shoulders.

'But I also heard him say he'd been born in some impossible year that hasn't happened yet.' She turned blank eyes on him, seeking his reassurance through the dimness. 'I think he was mad, wasn't he?'

'If he wasn't telling the truth,' Murray pointed out grimly, 'there's no rational explanation for all the things that happened, up to and including his dissolution.'

'Christ, that was so *horrible*!' The last word peaked to a moan of terror, and the teeth chattering resumed.

'Should have treated you for shock too, young woman,' Cromarty said. 'Try and control it till we get to my place. Not much further now.' He jutted his jaw forward as though clamping on the stem of the forgotten pipe.

'But tell me, Mr Douglas, since you seem to have made sense of the whole rigmarole – who was he?'

Murray sighed imperceptibly. Tomorrow it would all seem like a nightmare, with nothing to give it substance bar the memory of those who had endured it, and the few heat-twisted scraps of machinery salvaged from the ruins of Fieldfare House, as meaningless to contemporary science as the bio-electronic gimmickry Lester had been so scathing about.

Better so, perhaps . . .

He said in a rusty voice, 'As near as I can make out, some time in the future – the twenty-fifth century – they have advanced science that includes time-travel and the means of altering people's personalities using a field broadcast by a special triplem antenna like the one I found every night on my mattress. To satisfy the illegal cravings of some perverts, Valentine was organizing a supply of primitive people's experiences in recorded form, which could be played back to the purchasers and give them barbaric thrills – oh, compare it to cock-fighting in this country today. Banned, but some people enjoy it so much they don't care.

'His customers must be – going to be – oh, the hell with it. A pretty horrible bunch, anyhow, considering the sort of vicarious thrills Valentine had to provide. Who'd want to enter the mind of a relapsing alcoholic, for God's sake? And I think the task was only at the halfway stage, if that. It would have fitted the pattern if, a bit later on, Gerry had gone looking for his bottle of heroin after some dirty trick Delgado played on him, and found it had been taken away. Addiction to drugs, liquor, pornography, sexual kinks – and it was still only the start!'

He had to pause and swallow hard, before resuming his exposition with his eyes fixed unseeing on the dark roadside.

'But it's difficult enough merely to translate something from one language to another and be sure you're understood. It must have proved much worse trying to present the experiences of people far in the past to the – well – the modern mind. So Delgado hit on the idea of taping the experiences of actors; as he said, they live half their lives in other people's minds anyway. And this worked, and made fortunes for Valentine and his gang.

'To make the most of their fairly limited opportunities, they deliberately encouraged unstable people to rub one another up the wrong way and heighten the emotions recorded. If I hadn't interfered, they'd have got me down as a hopeless alcoholic –'

'And me as a fullblown Les,' Heather said. 'It's so frightening, Murray! They said "the urge was on her tapes" and if you hadn't worried me so much I cut the wire every night it would have worked, and I'd have been seduced by Ida and then someone who hasn't even been born yet would – would –'

'This is carrying voyeurism a step too far,' Cromarty said with an attempt at light relief. It was a ghastly failure. 'But it might not have worked, young woman!'

'It would have,' she said obstinately. 'There's a bit of it in all of us – you should know that, as a doctor. I used to get crushes on older girls when I was at school, so it's probably still in me, just below the surface, waiting for –'

Hysteria on the way, Murray diagnosed, and wondered if he was going to have to slap her face to quiet her. But at that moment the car slowed, and there ahead was the gate of Cromarty's home. A curtain moved at an upper window. Lights came on. The housekeeper Murray had met before appeared to let them in.

She exclaimed in horror over Heather's condition and led her away with promises of a hot bath and a comfortable bed, while Cromarty brought Murray his own thick woollen dressing gown and slippers that were much too big. In the surgery, he tended in silence to the burns on his feet. It was not until new bandages were in place that he glanced up from under his greying brows and put the key question.

'Mr Douglas, do you *really* believe what the man Delgado said?'

'Ask me tomorrow,' Murray said wearily.

'Yes, of course.' Distressed, Cromarty jumped up. 'I'm sorry, I should let you go straight to bed. Not much of a bed, I'm afraid. Mrs Garbett has probably given the young lady the one I meant to offer you when I suggested your coming here, but we'll see what we can do . . . Mrs Garbett!'

26

A shrilling noise. Instantly he was awake and terrified, thinking of the phone beside his bed and the hateful greasy voice of Valentine telling him that it was breakfast time. He was on his feet before he realized that was past and over.

Relief made him collapse limply on the edge of the – not bed: a big settee in the doctor's drawing room, of course, where they'd made him up a pallet of rugs and cushions last night. Outside bright sunlight. An early bee buzzing. Oh, this was a miracle!

He checked his watch, and saw with puzzlement that it read one-twenty. Stopped when Valentine knocked him down last night? With one hand he touched his head gingerly, with the other shook the watch before putting it to his ear.

Going all right. So –

There was a tap at the door, and the smiling face of Mrs Garbett appeared. 'It's all right, Doctor, he's awake!' she threw over her shoulder, and continued to Murray, 'Good morning, Mr Douglas – or afternoon, I should say. Dr Cromarty thought it best you should be left to sleep yourself out after what you've been through.'

'I – oh, then it is twenty past one.' Murray thrust back his sleep-tousled hair. 'I'm sorry if I've been a nuisance.'

'A nuisance? Bless you, sir, after what you did last night – it's in the paper and I read it twice – you deserve anything we can give you. There's someone to see you, or I'd not have come in.'

Someone to see me? Then the doorbell was what woke me. Murray felt a great deal of satisfaction in establishing the fact. Before he could speak again, to ask what all this was about the papers, Mrs Garbett had stepped aside and there in her place was Roger Grady, face white with concern, coming forward at a rush.

'Christ, Murray, am I glad to see you! When I heard the news at breakfast-time I dropped everything. Can you ever forgive me for not taking you seriously when you rang last night?'

'Just a moment,' Murray said slowly. 'What news did you hear?'

'About Fieldfare House burning down and your rescuing all those people!' It was Roger's turn for a blank expression.

'But how did that get in the papers? It was so late that –'

'Not too late for the London editions, which come out at least as far as this. Someone should have told – oh, of course, you've slept the whole morning. Anyhow, I heard it on the radio, and then after I spoke to Sam –'

'You what?' Murray put up a hand feebly. 'You're going too fast for me – my God – *Sam!* What are you doing here? You're supposed to be in hospital!'

'Nothing wrong with me,' grunted the director. He had been standing in the doorway waiting to be noticed. 'When I found out what had happened I told them anyone who stopped me coming here to thank you would get a poke in the eye.'

'Sam rang me to try and find out what had become of you,' Roger amplified. 'No one at the hospital knew, apparently – and fortunately for your rest, they therefore couldn't tell any reporters. What's this?'

'Here you are, sir,' Mrs Garbett was saying, waving the morning paper at him. 'In the *Stop Press*, it is. "Actor in Fire Drama. Fire swept Fieldfare House, Bakesford, where company in rehearsal for new Delgado play, two a.m. All in house were asleep except Murray Douglas, well-known actor, who gave alarm and carried to safety members of cast overcome by smoke. Three fire brigades called."'

'Anybody dismissing it as a Delgado-inspired publicity stunt?' Murray said bitterly after a pause.

'As a matter of fact, yes,' Roger said with some embarrassment. 'I don't suppose I have to tell you who.'

'Still smarting from that sock in the jaw?'

'Apparently.'

'Well, he's not going to get away with it!' Blizzard barked. 'I'm going to his editor this afternoon, and if he bleats one snide word in his column tomorrow I'll have him barred from every theatre in the country, I swear it. Ah – Murray.' His voice dropped. 'I guess I owe you not merely thanks, but an apology. I don't know what Delgado was up to, not yet, but one thing stands out a mile. He was doing something abominable to us. *Must* have been. All of us, snoring blithely away while the house was on fire? It just isn't possible, I don't *believe* it. I didn't even wake up in the ambulance, or when they put me to bed in the hospital – none of us did. We were sleeping like the dead. And that's what we could have been.

'I was taken in by Delgado, that's the plain truth.'

'He was a genius. Or at least his tapes made him one.'

'What?' Blizzard said, bewildered.

'Skip it,' Murray sighed. 'Anyway, much as I appreciate your kind words, I'd rather have some breakfast and get some clothes from somewhere –'

'I brought some,' Roger interrupted eagerly. 'In the car, a bagful. I'll fetch them. You're near enough my size, though I don't know about shoes.'

He vanished hastily. Blizzard, though, stood his ground. 'Murray, you're not going to slide out of it. And I'm not going to waste the money and effort I sank into these weeks of work. I'm going to finish this job, and the hell with Delgado – let him rot in his grave along with his damned tape-decks and sleep-teaching gimmicks.'

'He's rotted already,' Murray said.

Blizzard checked. 'Someone said something about that, at the hospital. Said he was brought to the mortuary in a sort of puddle, as though his flesh had melted off his bones. But it sounds crazy.'

'Just be glad that you're not. Another couple of weeks, and you wouldn't have had a play. You'd have had a spectacle to make the *Marat-Sade* look like a Christmas pantomime.' Murray stretched and rose.

'I'm going to have a play,' Blizzard said doggedly. 'And it's going to put your name back where it belongs, at the head of the list. It's the least I can do. I believe every accusation you laid against Delgado now. I believe he tried to frame you into seeming drunk, I believe he got those damned stewards to cover up for him – the sod was playing with our lives like a Punch-and-Judy man. Making us wallow in dirt and then boast about it!' His face was red with his vehemence.

Murray was going to correct the mistaken assumption about the 'stewards', but changed his mind. What was the point, anyway? He said absently, 'Not right away, though – hm?'

'Of course not. We've lost the house and its theatre. But the insurance will cover it, and between us we can recreate the outline we had and the dialogue too. Anyway, we shan't get the Margrave after all, thanks to Patsy pulling strings, but the New Brecht has offered us a season in two months if we're available, and I wouldn't object to a pre-London run, frankly.'

Murray was hardly listening. Physically, he was much better, but his whole mind was pervaded with illimitable weariness. There would be time later for matters like salvaging the play, sorting out the finances, and related problems. Right now there was only one point he had to make.

'If you're seriously going on with it,' he said, and waited.

'Damnation, am I going to throw away all this work – not to mention the money?' roared Blizzard.

'Then remember Heather, won't you? You know why Delgado wanted her around, I hope?'

'I think I've figured that out this morning,' Blizzard agreed. 'To – uh – to amuse Ida. Not for her own sake.'

'Correct.' Murray's eyes had roved to the window; here was Roger coming back again, carrying a bulging travelling bag. 'Well, she's going to be in the production if I have to write a part for her myself.'

'I was going to ask you,' Blizzard said. 'Thinking back, I realized we owed a good half of the material to your suggestions, and –'

Murray wasn't listening. He had pulled on Dr Cromarty's dressing gown and gone into the hallway, ignoring Roger at the front door with the bag of clothes. 'Mrs Garbett! Mrs Garbett! Where did you put Heather?'

And the hell with any susceptibilities you may have.

'In the room on the right at the top of the stairs, Mr Douglas,' the housekeeper called demurely. 'I don't know if she's awake yet, but I was just going to take her a cup of tea and –'

She appeared with a laden tray. There were two cups on it. Murray took it from her with a skeletal grin and started up the stairs, favouring his sore feet equally.

But the pain seemed to belong to the past, and he was heading for the future. Like it or not.

True or false? A madman's raving, a tissue of lies told by a twisted genius, or cold appalling fact?

Never mind. Let the dead bury their dead, in or out of time. For him, at this moment and with luck forever, it was enough that in Delgado's death he had found his own life anew. The idea was still strange, but it was comforting. He tapped on the door to which he had been directed, went in, and closed it behind him.

Other titles by John Brunner

The Squares of the City†

'*The Squares of the City* is a first-class fantasy thriller that will hold the reader through to its disturbing climax – a climax that poses serious questions about how and to what degree man is to be governed and whether potentially bloody conflicts can be resolved by subterfuge without morally denigrating all mankind' – *New York Times*

Telepathist

Gerald Howson was hopelessly and hideously crippled: a runt who shuddered at the sight of his own face. But he was the greatest curative telepathist in the world: the world's most irreplaceable person. He could 'project' six thousand miles and undo the knots in a man's mind. He could have anything he wanted except the life that only Rudi could give him . . .

The Long Result

It sounds ideal. Americans, Eskimos, Rumanians and Spaniards working side by side. Sharing a common language and a common purpose – cosmic civilization.

But there's still room for racists. Even if it means killing, The Stars Are For Man League is determined to keep mankind supreme among the alien life-forms . . .

This is a new departure in S.F. – *galactic politics.* And all forms of life have a stake in the outcome.

Not for sale in the U.S.A.
†Not for sale in Canada and the U.S.A.